A Spark of Romance

A Spark of Romance

Jamie K. Schmidt

TULE
PUBLISHING

A Spark of Romance
Copyright© 2020 Jamie K. Schmidt
Tule Publishing First Printing, June 2020

The Tule Publishing, Inc.

First Publication by Tule Publishing 2020

Cover design by Elizabeth Mackey

ISBN: 978-1-967678-15-0

Acknowledgments

I'd like to thank Assistant Chief Michael Shove, from the Guilford Fire Department, and former volunteer firefighter Michael Clemente, for helping me research and answer all of my questions.

Thank you for your time and your service to our community.

Any mistakes are all mine, though.

Chapter One

T HE LONG DRONE of the fire horn shattered the peace of the dawn, the noise rippling over the still waters of Long Island Sound. Kayleigh Baker and her youngest sister, Leah, exchanged looks and began to rapidly reel in their lines.

"Sorry about this," Kayleigh said. She was the fire chief in their small town of Mulberry, Connecticut, and even if she wasn't on duty, Leah knew she couldn't sit still on the boat and wonder what was going on.

"That's fine. The fish weren't biting anyway. I was snoozing with my line in."

A second horn went off, followed by a third, and then a fourth. It was a big fire and EMS was needed.

"How quick can you get me back?"

"Depends on if there are any kayakers out." Leah flashed Kayleigh a grin. "Help me with the anchor."

As Leah started up the motor, Kayleigh sprinted up to the bow of the ship and started hauling up the anchor chain, hand over hand. "Tell me again, why you don't have this on a winch?"

"I did. It broke."

After their mom's death almost a decade ago, Leah had

taken over Mulberry Fishing Tours. The boat had seen better days, but Leah would never even consider a new one. Too many good memories of their mother and their childhood were wrapped up in this boat.

With a tug and a grunt, Kayleigh brought the anchor aboard. She had just secured it when her sister put the boat into gear and punched it.

"Hold on," Leah said.

Kayleigh wobbled on the bow, years of practice keeping her from losing her balance. Old as it was, the fishing boat could still move. And there wasn't anything Leah liked better than letting the throttle loose. Muttering under her breath about reckless boat drivers, Kayleigh grabbed hold of the canopy frame that kept Leah's customers from getting too much sun, and swung herself back into the cabin area. The roar of the twin engines and the spray of the waves made her heart beat fast as the boat bounced toward the harbor. Kayleigh enjoyed it when the boat was going full speed too. It felt like flying. She couldn't keep the grin off her face. This was the reason she came back to Mulberry and she needed to remember that when she got restless about staying in one place for too long.

Blazing by the No Wake signs, Leah expertly maneuvered the boat toward the dock. There weren't any kayakers out, thank goodness. Otherwise, the waves they'd created would have really tested the paddlers' bracing skills.

"Back it down," Kayleigh said.

"Don't tell me how to drive."

"You're going to give Burt a heart attack." Burt was the

dockmaster. He was storming down the pier to where Leah's berth was.

"I need a siren," Leah said. "Don't you think I need a siren?"

"Yeah, that's exactly what you need." With practiced ease, Kayleigh flipped over the bumpers to protect the side of the boat as Leah slowed down, so Kayleigh could jump off at the dock.

Burt was already standing on the end of the dock, hands on his hips, glaring at them. Cigar sticking out of his mouth, he grabbed the rope Kayleigh tossed at him to help keep the boat from drifting away. Leah idled it and gave him a little wave.

"I'm going back out," she said.

"You're lucky this is an emergency. I'd have your license for coming in like that." He pointed his finger at her. "Keep it under six mph in the harbor area."

Leah smiled innocently at him and batted her eyelashes. "Okay, Burt."

He grunted in disgust, obviously not buying her act. He had known them both since they were born, since he'd been one of their mother's closest friends. The crusty old seaman was all bark and no bite—unless you were from out of town and not following the rules.

"I'll see you later," Kayleigh said. "Thanks for the help, Burt." She clapped him on the back as they started up the ramp to the parking lot.

Leah turned the boat around and went back out at a much more sedate pace.

"Have you been listening to the radio?" Kayleigh asked him.

Burt nodded. "It's a bad one. Ambulance took away the whole family for smoke inhalation. Your guys are still duking it out with the fire. It's a hot one, and they're worried about it spreading."

"Thanks for the heads-up." Kayleigh sprinted for her car, jumped in, and turned on the siren. After plugging in her phone, she called into dispatch to find out where the fire was, and was told it was in the Lake Hills area of town, where the big mansions looked down on a man-made lake. In the Hills, away from the small farms and the harbor area, the residents could pretend they were their own village. But they were just as much a part of her jurisdiction as the residents who lived down in the Harbor in smaller cottages and apartments.

The sun was just coming up and the chill of the dawn would soon fade away into a hot June day. Kayleigh could smell the smoke and see the orange red nimbus cloud of fire as her car climbed up the hills.

She wasn't surprised to find Police Chief Liam MacAvoy there with his team, keeping a perimeter, so the gawkers and media trucks couldn't get in the way of the firefighters. Liam had light brown hair, trimmed neat and efficiently, but he could do nothing about his chronic five-o'clock shadow. He was lean and muscular and kept in shape by teaching kids martial arts on the weekend. Even though he was a black belt in tae kwon do, she never saw him showing off by breaking boards or anything like that. She liked that he was humble and not flashy. He was tall and handsome in a boy-next-door kind of way, and when she stared at him for too long, she lost all sense. Their eyes met as she stepped over the crime-scene tape, and she raised her eyebrow at it. He gave her a tight nod, his gaze cold and flinty, as she shook her head at what it meant.

They didn't need to speak to understand each other. They had grown up together in this town. He was from the Lake Hills area and she was from the Harbor, but the class difference hadn't bothered them. Not when they'd been in school anyway. In fact, back then, they had been best friends. Along with Evan Johnson, who was now the town's first selectman, they had been inseparable like The Three Musketeers.

Or as her mother had put it, "the three monkeys," because they'd always been swinging around trees and getting into trouble for being rowdy.

It hadn't gotten messed up between them until high school, when Liam had taken their pranks a bit too far and kissed her. Kayleigh was furious that he used her unrequited crush for him against her. After that, things had gone downhill—not only in their friendship, but in their lives as well. And then she went off to Iraq, and everything changed.

She had spent ten years trying to forget all about Mulberry and the pain of her mother's death. But she couldn't run away forever; so now she was back, and the guilt and memories hadn't gone away. Liam and Evan had stayed in Mulberry waiting for her, and she'd spent the last year and a half trying to come to terms with them.

Shaking off her mood, Kayleigh hurried over to the truck where her fire captain, Hank Stewart, was in control of the situation. She'd gathered, from Liam's expression, that this had been arson. That would explain why the fire was so hot and hard to control.

"They used an accelerant." Hank sounded tired and dejected.

"How's the family? I heard they were transported to the hospital."

"They're going to be all right. Well, the wife and kids are. The husband confessed to hiring people to set the house on fire for the insurance money. But the thugs got the dates wrong. They should have waited until next week when the family was on vacation."

Kayleigh whistled low. Nothing people did surprised her anymore. If her years in the army hadn't taught her that, her time as a firefighter had. She got into her gear and waded in to give one of her crew a break.

LIAM'S EYES WERE drifting closed, and he got out of his car to stretch so he wouldn't be caught napping on duty. Mulberry was a sleepy little town—except when it wasn't—and he'd tried hard not to become the stereotype of a police chief, like his father had been.

The day had started out terrible with the fire that Kayleigh and her team had managed to keep from spreading. No one was seriously injured, thank goodness, but the house was a goner. And he had the unhappy privilege of arresting one of his mother's neighbors for committing a felony. All in all, it had been a busy day, and it wasn't even noon yet.

He'd been happy to see Kayleigh, though. Not that they'd had any time to talk. She had looked good, probably having just come off her sister's boat. Kayleigh was as tall as he was and built muscled and sturdy. She worked hard and played even harder. When they'd been in high school, she'd wanted to play football. She was a heck of a defensive tackle, but her mom had yanked her off the team because she'd been afraid Kayleigh would get hurt. They'd compromised on ice hockey. It wasn't any less dangerous, but her mom trusted the safety gear more.

Kayleigh was also drop-dead gorgeous and had no idea he'd been in love with her for most of his life. The first time Liam had asked her out, it had gone so badly, he'd never done it again. He should have known she wouldn't be interested in a guy like him. Too boring. Too much of a small-town kid with roots in the place she was dying to get out of. When she'd left for the army right after high school, Liam had thought he'd missed his chance with her. However, after a few tours in Iraq and working as a firefighter up and down the East Coast, Kayleigh had come back home with a Bronze Star, a Purple Heart, and a thousand-yard stare that made him wonder if the girl he knew was gone forever. Still, she'd been back two years now, and it looked like Kayleigh was finally putting down roots. It gave him some hope.

Liam was a little stiff from standing all morning at the

crime scene, so even though it was a good decade since his beat-patrol days, he decided to walk around the neighborhood that had been experiencing a rash of car thefts. He didn't expect to find anything out of the ordinary in the daylight, but maybe some insight would hit him. Besides, it would be good public relations for the town to see him out there.

Most of the robberies had taken place at night, while the owners were sleeping. The thieves would park and then go into the driveways on foot. Liam had some blurry security photos of men and women in hoodies trying car doors. If they were locked, the thieves moved on. If they weren't . . . well, sometimes Mulberry's residents had to be reminded not to leave their purses and laptops in their cars overnight.

As Liam turned the corner, he did a double take. Yes, there in broad daylight, was a white man in his late thirties, wearing sunglasses and a hoodie, attempting to jimmy open a car door with a wire coat hanger. Deciding to investigate, Liam approached the man slowly, coming up on his blind side.

Mulberry was a small town, but not so small that Liam knew everyone in it. It could be that this was the owner and he'd locked his keys in his car. But as Liam watched, it was apparent that wasn't the case because the man kept looking around furtively and hunkered down when a car passed the driveway. Liam toggled the microphone on his collar.

"Dispatch, I've got a 459 in progress." Liam quietly gave the address.

"Do you need assistance, Chief?"

The thief took that moment to look up and saw him standing there.

"Don't run," Liam said.

The man took off.

"I hate it when they do that. Yeah, send a car as backup." Liam sprinted after the man.

Another thing he hadn't done in over a decade was run track, but as the perp jumped over hedges and tipped over lawn chairs behind him, Liam found himself hurdling over the objects as if his glory days in track had been yesterday.

"Stop! You're under arrest!" He panted, not expecting it to work, but he had to try. While he still had breath, Liam called in the man's description and location. He should have driven around the neighborhood instead of running full out with the extra weight of his gun belt around his waist. He was a stroller, not a sprinter. "Too much time behind your desk," he muttered.

Kayleigh would have caught the perp by now. Hell, the guy probably wouldn't have even run from her. Of course, Kayleigh might have shot him the moment he fled. She was impulsive that way, believing that the best way to stop a fight was to end it before it started.

It had gotten her into a lot of trouble in high school. Their JROTC instructor had tried to drill procedure into her head, but in the end, he claimed she wasn't officer material and forced her out of the program. Liam should have stood up for her, but he'd been too afraid of what his parents would have said if he'd been thrown out too.

Liam, of course, had never broken the rules in high

school and had graduated top of his class. Unfortunately, his father hadn't made it to see him graduate. A heart attack took him quickly and quietly as he was getting out of his squad car. So, instead of going away to college and continuing on with ROTC, Liam had chosen to stay in Mulberry to take care of his mother. He'd always wondered how his life might have been different if he'd gone to boot camp with Kayleigh like they'd planned.

The perp looked over his shoulder and spotted that Liam was gaining on him. Cursing, the would-be thief darted into the street, narrowly missing getting hit by a car. Liam followed, flashing his badge, but maneuvering through the cars slowed him down.

"Freeze!" he shouted. Again, he hadn't expected it to work. He was starting to get shin splints, but he wasn't going to let his only burglary lead get away. Ignoring the discomfort, he dug in and continued with the chase. This running stuff was for the birds.

As Liam gained once more on the suspect, they exited the rural neighborhood. The thief was headed toward the commuter parking lot, but Liam couldn't let him get to his car. Putting on an extra burst of speed, he leapt in the air and tackled the guy, trying his best to land them both on grass instead of the pavement.

"Police brutality. Police brutality!" the man yelled.

Liam wrestled the thief until he could secure the man's wrists behind his back. He was hauling the perp to his feet when two squad cars pulled up. They were a little late, but at least he wouldn't have to walk back to his car.

"I told you not to run," Liam gasped out. His legs were jelly and he had a stitch in his side that made him want to double over in pain, but no one had to know that.

On the outside, he was the police chief his father would have been proud of, a man Kayleigh could look up to. On the inside, though, Liam wondered if Kayleigh was better off with someone more adventurous, a guy who hadn't lived his whole life in Mulberry.

Chapter Two

KAYLEIGH WALKED INTO Baker and Daughters Auto Shop with a six-pack of bottled birch beer soda in one hand and a large white clam pizza in the other. Friday night pizza and birch beer were a tradition in the Baker family. Six p.m. sharp. She knew better than to be late, but her sisters were already there and their father had started eating without her. Leah had brought a tomato pie, which was her dad's favorite. It was a pizza topped with crushed San Marzano tomatoes, grated pecorino Romano cheese, and olive oil.

"It's a giant cracker," Kayleigh said, shaking her head at it. "It's not a pizza unless you have cheese."

"No, it's not a pizza unless it has tomato sauce," Samantha said. She wiped her hands on a greasy rag, before sitting down at the table. Samantha was the middle child and took great pleasure in ribbing both her sisters equally. As always, her job was to stock the freezer with lemon and raspberry Italian ice for dessert.

The pizza argument was an old one. They'd all eat whatever pizza was in front of them until it was gone. It was just a comfortable tradition that Kayleigh hadn't realized she'd missed until she came back to Mulberry.

"How's Daisy?" Kayleigh nodded toward Samantha's

VW bug, which was up on the hoist.

"Timing belt." Samantha made a sour face.

Kayleigh winced in sympathy. Jules Baker had trained all of his girls to work on cars. Each one them could have been a mechanic, but the only one who'd gone into the family business was Samantha. Leah had wanted to be a fishing boat captain, like their mother. And Kayleigh had just wanted out of this town. Without college money, the army had been her best choice—she had headed out for boot camp the day after graduation. And when her mother passed, she'd been in Iraq. No one had been able to reach Kayleigh until her unit returned from their mission several weeks later. She'd never forgiven herself for missing her mother's funeral. She didn't regret her time in the army, but if Kayleigh had to do it all over again, there were things she would have done differently. Like finding a part-time job so she could go to college first. Had she done that, she would have been closer when her mother had succumbed to an aneurysm.

Setting the pizza and soda down at the picnic table outside of the shop, Kayleigh sat next to her father. Jules hadn't looked up from his phone since she arrived. She had set him up with his own Facebook account because he had wanted to know what the big deal was about social media. And now, they couldn't get him off it.

"Phone down," Leah said, joining them at the table. She handed out paper plates and napkins.

"Busy day in Mulberry." Jules reluctantly put the phone facedown on the table. "First the fire, and now I hear that they caught one of the thieves who has been breaking into cars in the area."

"Good," Samantha grunted, reaching for the clam pizza. Using her finger, she scooped up a dollop of ricotta cheese that fell off and landed in the box.

"I heard our very own police chief ran him down and tackled him." Leah grinned.

Kayleigh choked on her birch beer. "Liam?"

"I would have paid cash money to see that," Samantha said.

"You and me both." Kayleigh grabbed the last slice of the clam pizza before Leah could snatch it from her.

"Someone had to have had their camera out." Jules reached for his phone.

"Dad," the three of them said in warning.

"Fine," he huffed.

They started in on the second pizza. While it lacked gooey mozzarella or ricotta cheese, Kayleigh could appreciate the sweet tomato taste mixed in with the smoky garlic.

"I posted some pictures of you girls and your mom on my page today."

"That's sweet, Dad. What's the occasion?" Kayleigh asked.

"It's getting close to Independence Day and I'm still not used to all the peace and quiet." Jules let out a shaky sigh. "It's been fifteen years since we lost her. Where did the time go?"

Kayleigh didn't have an answer for him. She wondered if the gaping wound in her family that had been left when Johanna Baker died would ever heal. Sometimes it seemed to be scabbed over, but this time of the year was always rough. That was part of the reason why Kayleigh had stayed away for so long. The summer memories had been more bitter than sweet.

The Fourth of July was big in her family, or at least it had been. Johanna Baker had loved fireworks. From the tiniest of sparklers to the monstrous twenty-four-inch shells that filled the sky with cascading, overlapping showers of light, their mother was a self-taught expert. She had started out lighting fireworks with flares and then graduated to rigging up triggers to car batteries. Toward the end of her life, she took more advanced electronics classes to put on a better show for her beloved town at the culmination of the summer festival, and the Bakers' official start of summer.

"I hope you put up the pictures of Kayleigh's show last year," Leah said.

"Better not have." Kayleigh gave her father the hairy eyeball.

It had been her first summer back in Mulberry—the first Fourth of July that Kayleigh had spent in town without her mother. She had wanted to put together a fireworks display in memory of her mother's beautiful shows. Good thing it had been in addition to the major display that the town had already planned to put on, because everything that could have gone wrong did. And it was also a good thing that she was the fire chief. She'd spent all day wiring up an elaborate show at the fairgrounds. But the expensive cakes had caught the field on fire. So, while it had been a decent pre-fireworks show, more people had been interested in the roaring blaze than the salutes and the dragon's egg that she'd dipped into her savings to purchase.

"This year will be different," Kayleigh vowed. "I've got it all planned out."

"Just make sure there are lots of water buckets," Samantha said.

"Is Evan going to let you try again this year?" Leah asked.

"Evan may run this town, but he knows better than to get in the way of a Baker and fireworks," Jules said.

"What about Liam? It was his squad car that got hit when one of the mortars tipped over."

Kayleigh closed her eyes. "No one was hurt. That was the main thing." She had told Liam not to park there, but he hadn't listened. She had wanted everyone back in a safe perimeter, but he had wanted to help light the fireworks the way he had when they'd been teenagers. And because she was a nostalgic idiot, she had let him. She should have made him move his car, but she had been too distracted, trying to figure out how to ask him on a date.

"It took months before he got the smell of burning leather out of his car." Samantha chuckled.

"I think there are still a few scorch marks," Leah added.

Kayleigh knew she had to nip this in the bud before it became a pig pile on her. "Don't worry. I'm letting the professionals handle the one this year. I'm just choreographing the display to some of Mom's favorite songs."

"That's nice," Samantha said.

"What's nice about it? We're all going to cry," Leah grumbled.

"No." Kayleigh shook her head. "Mom wouldn't have wanted that. She would have told us to yell and cheer at each big blast."

"She would have insisted she be there, lighting the fireworks herself, smelling the smoke, hearing the deafening roar." Jules looked up at the sky as if he could see them. "But she's not here. You don't have to do this for her."

"Yeah, the town might not survive another homemade display," Samantha said. "This time, do me a favor and aim for Evan's car."

Kayleigh and Leah exchanged looks. Samantha and Evan had dated for a few months, but it had gone nowhere. Apparently, Samantha was holding a bit of a grudge. Kayleigh would have to get more out of her sister about that later.

"It's all being done electronically this year. No more spare sparks landing on us. We'll all be at a safe distance." Kayleigh exchanged significant looks with her sisters. They had all been on the bucket brigade during their mom's shows, and they were all very well skilled in running while carrying two full, five-gallon buckets of water. "Tristar Fireworks is sending a rigger along with the truck and he's going to set us up. All I've got to do is coordinate the music."

"I can't wait to see it," Jules said. "I'm going to broadcast it live." He reached for his phone again.

They all rolled their eyes.

"Yeah, I'm sure your five followers, who will probably be at the show, will love it," Leah said, gathering up the garbage.

"It's still a few weeks away," Jules said. "I could go viral by then."

Kayleigh hoped not. The last time he tried to go viral, he had made Leah drop him off on one of the rocks in the harbor and shoot a video of him trying to get a brown seal to take a fish out of his hand. Instead, he almost drowned when a rogue wave took his feet out from under him. At least he'd had the sense to wear a life vest. Still, it had been a little too close a call for comfort.

AFTER CHURCH ON Sunday was family time, and Liam wanted nothing more than to take a nap on the couch. But his mother wasn't having any of it. While her cook made lunch, Lila MacAvoy was working on her favorite project—trying to marry Liam off.

"If you could have dinner with anyone in the world, who would it be?"

Liam knew better than to say Kayleigh Baker. Lila liked Kayleigh, but she didn't have the pedigree that his mother was looking for in his bride. Which was too darned bad, because he wasn't going to get married to improve his mother's social life, so he said, "Leonardo da Vinci."

His mother preened a little. "So cultured. Why?"

"Because he's dead and he wouldn't talk much."

"Liam," she groaned and slammed her hand on the couch. "Will you be serious?"

"No. Don't think I don't know you're trying to sign me up on dating sites with these questions. I told you. I'll find my own partners. I don't need your help."

"You need help, all right. I haven't seen you out on a date in forever."

"That's not true." Liam racked his brain to remember the last time he took someone out to dinner. It had been a while ago. She had been the daughter of one of the selectmen from the next town over. He had gotten a call during the middle of their evening and had to respond. There hadn't been a second date. "Besides, my life is pretty hectic right now."

Leaning back in the recliner, he kicked off his shoes and closed his eyes, hoping his mom would take the hint. For a moment, he thought he had succeeded.

"What do you value most in your personal relationships?" she said.

"Privacy." His father used to sleep after church all the time. Lila never would have bothered her husband with twenty questions. Although now that he thought about it, his father used to nod off in church. If Liam was being charitable, he could attribute the habit to his dad working long hours, but it was probably because his father had usually been drunk at ten in the morning.

"What's your most treasured memory?"

Kissing Kayleigh Baker by the lake, seconds before she cracked him across the jaw. It had been totally worth it.

"What are you smiling about?"

"Mom, how is this supposed to help me find a date?"

"Not a date," she said eagerly.

Liam opened up one eye.

"Your soulmate."

He sighed. "Are you reading those weird ladies' magazines again?"

"What do you mean 'weird'?"

"The ones where it shows how to lose ten pounds in one week on the cover right next to a picture of a four-layer cream cake you can make in the microwave. Then inside, it encourages you to get rid of clutter, while also showing you how to pick up great finds at tag sales."

"You've been reading them, too, I see."

"My phone battery died at the station, and I'd nothing else to read in the john."

"You need to get out more," she said. "All you do is work, work, work."

"I like my job."

"You almost died the other day chasing that criminal," she said, with a catch in her voice.

"No, I didn't."

"This job killed your father. I don't want the same thing happening to you."

"I'm pretty sure his three-pack-a-day habit and drinking problem contributed to his heart attack more than the stress of being Mulberry's police chief." Liam made it a point to neither smoke nor drink to excess, but he couldn't help that he loved being a cop.

"I need grandbabies," she wailed.

And that was the crux of it.

"Have you talked to Tammy lately?" Liam said, throwing

his older sister under the bus.

"Tammy is in California. You are right here. Would it kill you go out on a nice date with one of the founding families of Mulberry? Irene Mulberry is finally ready to start dating again after her husband died."

"Kill me? No." *Make me really uncomfortable, yes.* "You need a hobby. Why don't you apply to one of these dating sites yourself?"

"I'm too old," she grumbled.

"I'm not saying go on Tinder."

"What's that?"

"Never mind," he said. "There's got to be a meet-up group for senior citizens that you'd like."

"I hate knitting."

"So, don't knit." Liam rubbed a hand down his face. "I'm just throwing out some suggestions."

"I have my volunteer work and my committees. I'm fulfilled. I want you to be fulfilled too. It would make me so happy to see you settle down with someone in Mulberry."

"Me too," he said, his thoughts drifting to Kayleigh again.

"I'm happy we're on the same page."

Liam didn't think they were even in the same book, but he didn't want to argue.

The cook rang the bell and he hurried to the table. His favorite meal, fried chicken and potato salad, was being served for lunch.

"It smells delicious, Martha," he said, kissing her on the cheek. Martha had been with them all his life. She was like a second mother to him.

"Liam agreed to find a bride here in Mulberry and settle down. Isn't that wonderful?" Lila said.

"Yes, it is." Martha winked at him. "So, when's the wedding?"

"I've got to ask the girl first," he said.

Lila leaned forward, a shark scenting blood. "You've already picked someone?"

"It's still in the early stages. I don't want to jinx it." It had been more than fifteen years since their last kiss. Surely, it was safe for him to try to kiss Kayleigh again. Liam rubbed his jaw, remembering. His father wasn't around to screw it up and if his mother really wanted grandbabies, she'd keep her opinion about social stations to herself.

Lila held up her glass of sparkling water. "Let's have a toast."

"Let's not." Liam dug into the fried chicken.

As usual, his mother ignored him and handed Martha a glass. "To Liam and his girl."

Martha and Lila clinked glasses and drank.

Liam just continued to eat, hoping this would all blow over and give him some time to court Kayleigh without the whole town sticking their noses in—like last time. His father had wanted to arrest her for assault because she'd hit him. Her father had wanted to know just what Liam had done to warrant a slap.

It had been a nightmare.

But they were both adults now. It would be different this time.

At least, Liam *hoped* it would be different.

Chapter Three

KAYLEIGH HADN'T PLANNED on going out to the lake, but she wound up there anyway. Today was her day off and tomorrow she had to work twenty-four hours straight, so she wanted to get in as much outside time as possible. As she drove around, feeling the usual restlessness, she decided to go for a swim. But she didn't hit the beach. The salt water made her skin scaly and her hair a nightmare. The freshwater lake up in the Hills was much more appealing. And since the kids were still in school, once she was there, she was able to swim a few laps in makeshift lanes that the lifeguards put up without being disturbed.

Tired, but still restless, she swam to the middle of the lake and climbed onto the raft. Lying on the sun-weathered boards, Kayleigh threw her arm over her eyes. The raft rocked as someone else joined her. A wet body flopped down beside her.

"That was an easier swim when we were kids," Liam said, slightly out of breath.

Kayleigh turned on her stomach, not surprised to see him. He probably swam over from his side of the lake when he saw her. Resting her head in the cradle of her arms, she turned her head, and looked at him from half-closed eyes.

Watching the water drip off his muscled arms and legs was a good show. Even better, he was blissfully unaware that she was ogling him.

"A lot of things were easier when we were kids," she said. "Did anyone see you come out here?" Kayleigh looked around, but there didn't seem to be a crowd.

"Just the lifeguards."

This had always been their spot when they were growing up, but as the population grew and tourists came in, having the lake all to themselves was rare. Luckily, her job and his gave them days off in the middle of the week. But if anyone saw them out here, they wouldn't hesitate to come up to them and start talking about whatever problems they were having in town. And if Lila saw them, Kayleigh would have to deal with the same disapproving looks she used to dole out when they were kids.

Liam's mom had thought she was a bad influence. To be fair, Kayleigh had been.

"Don't suppose you brought any beer?" she asked lazily.

"What was I supposed to do? Bring it over strapped to my back?"

"Wouldn't be the first time," Kayleigh said.

"It's ten in the morning."

"Five o'clock somewhere," she muttered and closed her eyes, a little more at peace with him next to her. Some of the restlessness settled down when she was with him. It was one of the reasons she'd come back to Mulberry after nearly a decade of spending no more than two years in one place. The two-year mark was coming up for her stint in Mulberry and she wasn't sure if she wanted to stay or go.

Kayleigh just didn't know if there was anywhere left she could go where she wouldn't be haunted by memories. Memories of the war, of her mother, of Liam. Maybe after this fireworks show she could put her guilt to rest that she hadn't been there for her family when her mother passed. Scooting closer to the edge of the raft, she stared down into the murky depths of the lake, as if the answers she was looking for would be there.

"You know my mother's neighbors, the Delrays?" Liam asked, trailing water over her back.

She hissed, the water feeling cold on her sun-warmed back. Cupping her hand full of water, she splashed him. It turned into a water fight that landed them both in the lake. Kayleigh tried not to swallow water as she maneuvered around to dunk him from behind. He twisted and grabbed her close before pulling them both under. Luckily, she had a chance to take in a deep breath before they went underwater.

But below the lake's surface, the game was suddenly much different. They weren't kids anymore, with disapproving parents. The water fight had started out the way it always did, but this time, she was no longer squirming to get away from him. Her pulse fluttered and she realized she didn't need to breathe if it meant she wouldn't be held in his arms.

Liam kicked his legs and brought them to the surface. She climbed back onto the raft, glad that she could blame the sudden breathlessness on being underwater. When Liam joined her, she looked into his warm hazel eyes, wondering what she would see there. He had kissed her once on this raft, while they were watching the fireworks. She wondered if he would have the courage to do it again, especially after she'd cracked him one the last time he had tried it.

Kayleigh could swear she could hear the drips of water plinking off their bodies and hitting the raft. She wasn't sure how to breach the few inches that separated them, the few inches between friendship and something else. Did she even want to try for more if she wasn't sure she was going to stay in Mulberry? She wondered if he even thought of her that way.

"The Delrays," Liam said, breaking the expectant silence between them.

"Yeah." She looked away, the spell between them broken. "I remember them."

"They've got a new horse. It's a retired racehorse from Yonkers."

"Really?" She grinned. She hadn't been on a horse in ages.

"I think they're going to breed him."

Kayleigh shook her head. Harbor people took up clamming or putting out lobster pots to make money. Hills people bred racehorses. "It could work, especially if they want to open up the farm for tourists."

Liam made a face. "My mother would hate that."

"She could get in on the tourist traffic. Maybe have a roadside stand to sell her flowers."

"Or she could get Martha to do it."

"See if you can get a few shots of the horse for me. I'd love to see it."

"Just go up there yourself."

Kayleigh shook her head. "I don't know them that well. And you know how people up your way get."

Liam stiffened. "We're not all elitist snobs in the Hills."

"Not all, but enough that I don't want to risk stopping over uninvited." Kayleigh sat up. "They may call the cops on me if they saw my beat-up clunker pull in their yard, thinking I was there to rob them, like the guy you just caught."

"Different MO," Liam said. "Besides, I'm sure none of my crew would arrest you. Pretty sure anyway." He nudged her with his shoulder and the awkwardness was gone. They were friends. If she was going to stay in Mulberry, however, she wanted to be more than friends. She just wasn't sure how to go about it.

"Are you all set with prepping for the festival?" she asked. The summer festival was a few weeks away, but already everyone in town was hustling to get things ready. The anticipation was similar to the weeks before Christmas. This was one of Mulberry's major events. The planning committee started one week after the festival ended and it was a yearlong affair to pull the week of community building and fun together.

"What a nightmare that festival is." Liam groaned.

"Nightmare? I ought to toss you back in the lake." Kayleigh couldn't believe his attitude. It was like he had become the Grinch of Mulberry.

"You could try." His eyes sparked a challenge at her.

That was like waving a red cape in front of a bull, but she let it go. Mostly because she wasn't sure that she'd be able to win. But also, because she wanted to know what had made him say that about what was, in her opinion, the best thing about summer. "What's with the festival hate?"

He shook his head in disgust. "Last year?"

"I'm sorry about your car already."

"Not that. It's not just a small-town event anymore. The committee brought in vendors from New York City to sell knock-off purses. Illegal trademark infringements, right under our noses. Not to mention, there was an increase in pickpocketing, drunk and disorderly, and . . ." He looked away. "Injuries."

"That's just a small percentage of what happens. There are the tractor pulls and the hen-laying contests. The photography contest that, I have to point out, you won several years in a row."

He smirked. "That was a long time ago."

She shook his arm, trying not to notice the fine swell of muscle on it. "You need to remember the good times."

"Unfortunately, you're remembering a festival that hasn't existed in ten years," he said.

"Last year wasn't so bad. Me torching your car excluded."

"You're letting nostalgia blind you. The festival is good for the kids. But, for the adults, it's a pain in the neck. I'll be glad when it's over."

Kayleigh felt her anxiety spike. "I came back to Mulberry because it never seems to change. That's what made it easier for me to stay away—because I knew it would always be here for me."

"Things change and not always for the better," he said.

She nodded. "You don't have to tell me that."

Sighing, he grabbed her hand. "There are a few events that I'm looking forward to."

"Like what?" She was trying hard not to let the restlessness take over again. All she wanted to do was swim until she was too exhausted to think about how the town and everyone in it had moved on while she was getting her head together. His grip was warm and solid, though, and it centered her.

"Like kicking your butt in softball, and savagely defeating the firefighters in the chili-eating contest."

The old competitive spirit between them roused her back into wanting to toss him off the raft again. "In your best dreams."

"That'll give me something to look forward to while I'm drowning in permits and paperwork."

"This might be my last festival," she blurted out.

Liam closed his eyes. "Don't listen to me. I'm getting cranky in my old age. I don't mean to spoil your fun."

"I mean, I'm thinking of moving on."

His head jerked up. "You're leaving?"

"I'm not sure I belong here." She gave a half laugh. "I'm not sure I belong anywhere, though. That's the problem."

"Your family is here. Patty is here."

"Patty's got enough on her plate right now." Her best friend since kindergarten had gotten married shortly after Kayleigh got back to town and was about to give birth to her first child, so there hadn't been a lot of time for them to hang out. "My family has their own lives."

"The town needs you," Liam said quickly.

"Hank could step up if I left. I got lucky that old man Ritter chose me as his successor before he retired."

"A lot of folks would miss you if you left," he said.

"I'm not sure I'm even going to leave. Don't tell anyone?" she asked, leaning in.

"I won't."

"Thanks. You're a good friend." Kayleigh slipped into the water to do more laps. When she came back, tired from the punishing swim, Liam was gone.

Chapter Four

A few weeks later

LIAM DIDN'T HAVE to deliver the bad news to Kayleigh in person. It just gave him an excuse to spend time with her. He had hoped that by now, he'd have worked up the courage to ask her out on a date, but Liam didn't want the aggravation of listening to his crew and hers rag him about it if she shot him down. Not to mention, he still wasn't over the disaster of the first time he'd asked her out when they were kids. It had been bad enough that she hadn't believed he was serious.

His father had said within Kayleigh's hearing that it was for the best, and that she was probably just a gold digger playing hard to get. Twenty years later, Liam could still feel the shame washing over him. If the lake where they had been swimming had dragged him to the bottom, he would have gladly stayed there. Yeah, his family had money, but no one had ever accused them of having class.

Liam could barely look at Kayleigh for months afterward, until it finally all blew over. Small towns loved to fan the flames of vicious gossip and Liam thought his father's words would live beyond his grave. They did, but only in Liam's head—and quite possibly, in Kayleigh's.

No one even looked up from what they were doing as he parked his squad car and got out at the fire station. Stretching, he squinted into the firehouse, but he didn't see her. As he got closer, he heard her, though. Her voice echoed from deep inside the tanker truck's engine.

"Hand me the shop light." Half of her was underneath the hood. The other half was standing on a ladder. She reached out with a grasping hand behind her. Since no one else was around helping her, Liam went over and handed her the shop light.

"Thank you," she grumbled, clipping it next to her. "I need the torque wrench."

Searching around, Liam saw it half-buried among a pile of tools that had been haphazardly tossed in a bucket. Frowning, he handed her the wrench and started sorting through the tools, putting them in a neat and logical order.

"Spark plugs," she barked.

He handed her the box. "We have a mechanic in town, you know."

Kayleigh's body jerked and her head came up so fast, he thought she was going to bang it on the hood.

"I am a mechanic," she snarled. Her chocolate-brown hair was pulled back into a messy ponytail.

Liam hid a groan. "I know that. I'm just saying, your job isn't fixing trucks. It's your dad's."

She climbed down the ladder, wiping her hands on a rag, and he realized he'd stepped in it even deeper. "Are you here to tell me what my job is, Chief?" Her dark-brown eyes deepened to almost black when she was mad.

Chief. Not Liam. Yeah, he was in trouble.

"Can we just start over?" he said, holding up his hands in surrender. "I've got some bad news and I want to talk with you privately."

"Is everything all right?" Her pretty face went from annoyed to concerned in an instant. "It's not Lila, is it?"

"No, Mom's fine. Come out to my car, will you? I bought you a coffee."

"Oh, it's bad. Is it a mocha?"

He sighed and nodded.

Kayleigh gripped his arm. "Who died?"

He flexed and she snatched her hand away as if it burned. Smirking at her reaction, he said, "No one. Just get in the car."

They walked outside and Kayleigh squinted into the sun. "What time is it?"

"A little after eleven."

Rolling her neck, she rubbed a sore spot on her shoulder. "I've been working on that clunker all morning."

"At the risk of having my head bitten off again, why?" Liam opened the car door for her, and she slid in.

"Leave the door open," she said. "I could use the fresh air." That, and a couple of her guys had casually wandered outside to see what was going on. Kayleigh glared at them until they went back inside to mind their own business.

"Because every mechanic I talked to says she needs a new engine."

Liam snorted. "You need a new truck."

Peeling the lid off her coffee, Kayleigh took a deep, appreciative sniff and then a large sip. "Yeah, and you and I both know there's nothing in the budget for either one of those. So, I'm doing what I can to keep her from stalling out on us in an emergency." After another sip, and an awkward silence where Liam tried desperately to think of small talk, Kayleigh said, "Okay, I'm caffeinated enough to hear the bad news. Let me have it."

He was annoyed at the sense of relief he felt. This, he could do. He could report on the incident and they could discuss it. But he couldn't come up with anything less lame than *Hot out there, isn't it?* so, instead, he got down to business. "Tristar Fireworks got hit real bad by the flash floods this week."

She winced in sympathy. "I'm glad we didn't get that much rain."

"Well, it took out a great deal of their stock. Then, in the aftermath, their warehouse got broken into and looted. They don't have anything left."

"That's awful, but it's way out of your jurisdiction," she said. "It's two states away. Why are you involved? Do they think someone from Mulberry did it?"

"They don't have any suspects yet. But Mulberry is out twenty-five thousand dollars for the deposit on our fireworks. The insurance will eventually cover us, but we're out of luck for fireworks for the Fourth." The Fourth of July was a little over a week away and the town's annual summer celebration kicked off in a few days.

Kayleigh was already shaking her head. "It's inconvenient and a shame, but we still have the other half of that deposit

34

left. We'll just have to find another vendor to supply us. It'll be a smaller show, but it'll be better than nothing. I'll look into some of Mom's old contacts and see what we can get fast and cheap."

"Evan already asked around. The big shells are all sold out in the surrounding states." As the town's first selectman, Evan was both of their bosses, and even though the three of them grew up together, he didn't give them any special treatment. In fact, he went out of his way to make it look like he was above the "good old boy network." Normally, Liam appreciated that. But in this case, he wished Evan had been a little more conscientious of Kayleigh's feelings about the fireworks display. After last year's disaster, though, Evan was glad for any excuse to put the kibosh on the event.

Drinking more coffee, Kayleigh's eyes narrowed and her toes began to tap. "Then we'll go farther than the surrounding states. It's tradition. We end the summer celebration with fireworks on the Fourth."

"Not this year," Liam said.

She stared at him in shock, her expressive eyes wide with disbelief and hurt. "How can you say that? You, of all people, know how important the fireworks are to everyone in town."

Liam knew how important they were to her, and that was another reason he'd wanted to tell her the bad news in person. The fireworks display had been her mother's pet project. Johanna Baker had haggled, negotiated and designed the Mulberry fireworks shows as if they had been a "Fireworks by Grucci" production. But after she passed, interest had increasingly dwindled.

He shook his head. "Maybe when we were kids, but now it's all noise complaints and illegal displays. No one is going to miss them. And it saves the town money." Liam jerked his chin toward the tanker. "Maybe you can convince Evan to send some of it your way." It was better use of the town's funds anyway.

"I'm not going to do that. That's not what that money was budgeted for. I'm going to find a decent display for the remaining money we have. The show will go on." Kayleigh raised her coffee cup. "Even if I have to set it up myself."

He winced. Because that had gone so well last year. Why did she have to make this so difficult? "It's not going to go on. That's what I came here to tell you. Evan's already agreed to take it off the agenda for the summer celebration."

There was an explosion of silence in the car while he watched the range of emotions play across her face. Shock. Disbelief. Sadness. Anger.

Uh-oh.

"I think a lot of it has to do with what happened last year," Liam quickly said, trying to stave off the explosion.

Kayleigh looked down into her empty coffee cup. "I said I was sorry about your car." She licked her thumb and rubbed a mark on the dashboard that may or may not have been a soot stain from the mortar.

"Not that." He didn't like bringing up the subject of Chris, the twelve-year-old boy who had almost lost his fingers. It was painful to think about. Liam had been the one to find him and he could still hear the boy's cries in his nightmares.

It took Kayleigh a minute, but she could always read him easily. She put a comforting hand on his shoulder. He closed his eyes, wishing he could accept the comfort. Instead, he only felt guilt. He should have known Chris and his friends were up to something. He had seen them skulking around and his instincts had been pricked, but there had been too many things happening at once. And he hadn't got there until it was almost too late.

"That had nothing to do with the town's fireworks display," she said sadly. "Chris Danvers learned his lesson and has regained full use of his hand."

"But it could have been worse," Liam said. "The memory is still strong in the community and people aren't as excited about fireworks as they once were."

"They're not as eager to shoot off M-80s and bottle rockets in their backyards anymore either. And I think that's a good thing. It was a tragedy that Chris had to learn the dangers of fireworks the hard way, but that's why the public display is important. So these kids don't put on their own shows."

"I don't think we need to worry about that this year. What happened to Chris is still fresh in everyone's minds. Not to mention the fire and what happened to my car."

Kayleigh looked at him and he felt the force of anger in her gaze. "I told you to move it. Don't blame that on me."

"I think Mulberry needs to have a break from fireworks, that's all."

"We don't need a break. We need to make it fun and

safe again. You need to unclench and let yourself enjoy the week."

"I'm on duty. I'll unclench on my own time," he said. "We can find another way to close out the summer festival. Maybe movies on the beach. Just not *Jaws*. Unless you want to have people watch while dangling in inner tubes in the water. That could be fun. You and your sisters could put on snorkel equipment and pull on people's legs," Liam joked, trying to defuse the situation, but he knew it was pointless. He should have found a better way to break it to her.

"I don't believe this," she whispered.

"It's just a fireworks show." He covered her hand with his.

She jerked hers away and ran it over her head, smoothing the stray hairs that escaped her ponytail. "You, of all people, should know better than to say that to me."

He sighed. It was just one day. It was not even a day. It was less than an hour of bright lights and big noises. But if he put it to her like that, she probably never would speak to him again. Kayleigh equated the fireworks show with keeping her mother's memory alive. That was what had started last year's travesty. But anyone who knew Johanna Baker would never forget her.

"Our teams could use the time off. Let them relax and celebrate summer with their families," Liam said. Ever since she'd mentioned that she might be moving on, he had been racking his brain trying to find out what would make her stay. Now would be a good time to suggest that she could hang out with him that night.

"I can't believe you and Evan made this decision without me."

Or not.

"Technically, the flash floods and the looters made the decision." Liam tried for another joke, but it also fell flat.

"This isn't over." Kayleigh crumpled the empty cup in her fist. "Don't get rid of your extra shift for that night. Mulberry's fireworks show will go on."

Chapter Five

KAYLEIGH STARED OUT the window at the kids hanging out on the town green. Some of them had super soaker water guns. A few others were playing Frisbee, and another group was engaged in some form of capture the flag. School had just gotten out for the summer and Mulberry's summer celebration was kicking off with a softball tournament tomorrow.

Mulberry hadn't changed much in the years she had been gone. That was part of the charm of it. The town green was the hub of excitement. It was surrounded by churches and small boutiques. The green itself was a large park. Spanning twelve acres, people walked their dogs around it, or just sat on the park benches and watched the town go by. A short stroll from the green were the beach and the docks, along with restaurants that served seafood fresh off the boat.

Kayleigh's own last day of high school seemed as if it had been only a few weeks ago. She had been excited to start boot camp, go travel the world, and then have the army pay for her college education.

Back then, Kayleigh should have enjoyed being eighteen and free without any responsibilities. But she wasn't wired like that. Kayleigh got antsy sitting around doing nothing, which is why waiting outside First Selectman Evan Johnson's office was driving her slowly up the wall. She turned to glare across the waiting area to where Liam sat, staring intently at his phone. Would it kill him to talk with her? They didn't even have to discuss the fireworks or his casual indifference to them.

Did he even remember that they'd had their first kiss under the blast of a red, white, and blue chrysanthemum explosion? Of course, what happened afterward was too cringe-worthy to dwell on. His rich parents didn't like him slumming with the mechanic's daughter from the Harbor. It had put a damper on their friendship for a while. But Liam had never cared about money or class differences, so after a few awkward moments, they had gotten back to normal.

He had to remember her mom taking them out on the boat to see the fireworks from the ocean. Johanna Baker had loved the summer and the coastal town of Mulberry that brought in literal boatloads of tourists every year. She had run boat tours around the surrounding small islands off the coast. The Thimble Islands were a popular spot for day cruises and, with certain permits, one could visit Faulkner's Island, which was a wildlife preserve and a bird sanctuary. After Johanna's death, Leah had expanded the business— adding fishing trips up and down Long Island Sound—and was doing quite well.

How could Liam have forgotten how much fun they'd had during the summer festival? And how much the tradition still meant to the small town they lived in? She needed to feel normal again. Kayleigh thought that by being back home, all that would come back. But, sometimes, she still woke up thinking she was in Iraq, and overwhelming dread would hit her until she realized she was back in Mulberry. Having another shot at the fireworks display—making it a blazing tribute to her mom—would go a long way in helping her settle back into her skin and start enjoying small town life again. If it didn't drive her crazy first.

Getting up from her chair, she paced back and forth.

Liam raised an eyebrow. "Do you have ants in your pants?"

If that had come from anybody but Liam MacAvoy, she would've invited them to check themselves. But because they were community leaders in the middle of town hall, it probably wasn't the best comeback line. Especially since a part of her wondered if he'd recoil in horror at the suggestion. Aside from that one kiss, he had always treated her as one of the guys. Of course, he hadn't been serious when he kissed her. Still, everyone in town had an opinion about them dating. And when the rumors about what they had really been doing ran wild, it just became too much. They had only been swimming, but the gossip grew like a game of telephone.

In the last version she had heard, they had been caught in a compromising position and their fathers had gotten into a fist fight. Shaking her head, she remembered how mortified she and Liam had both been. It served him right for not being serious about kissing her.

"I don't know what the big wait is about. We had a one o'clock appointment," she said.

"It's only seven minutes past," he replied laconically.

She wished she had one of the squirt guns the kids were playing with. She'd love to send a volley of water at Liam. Maybe he'd look up from his phone and notice her. Kayleigh snorted. *Yeah, and maybe pigs would fly.*

"Evan probably got delayed on a phone call, or maybe a meeting ran long."

Blowing out a sigh, Kayleigh sat down next to him, probably too close for his comfort, but he didn't move away. He was working on a crossword puzzle on his phone. "How come you didn't respond to my Scrabble Battle invite, if you like word games so much?"

"My ego's too fragile," Liam said, his voice deadpan. "You'd probably kick my butt, and then I wouldn't be able to look you in the eye."

"You're not looking me in the eye anyway."

Liam put down his phone and turned to her. She was struck by the green flakes in his hazel eyes. They were entirely too close. In fact, they are almost nose to nose. Should she fake a sneeze or something to break the awkward silence between them? Could this be attraction? Something more than just annoyance? Before she could say or do anything, the first selectman opened the door. They sprang apart as if they'd been kissing instead of just staring soulfully into each other's eyes. *That did not just happen.* She was letting wishful thinking get the best of her again.

Yanking down on her shorts, she got up and felt, rather than saw, Liam uncoil himself from his chair. Kayleigh could sense his presence behind her, and it made her want to do something juvenile, like stop short or jab an elbow back into his chest. Then things would be comfortable, familiar again. But they weren't kids anymore. They were adults, and for the past year, they'd worked side by side helping the Mulberry community in their respective public service jobs.

"So, my secretary tells me that this is about the fireworks display." Evan sat on the edge of his desk. His suit looked rumpled and he had a salsa stain on his tie, probably from eating standing up at the taco truck.

Mmmm . . . tacos.

"I want you to know I'm against it," Liam said, breaking her out of her taco moment.

"Brownnoser," she muttered under her breath.

He hip-checked her as he went to take a seat in one the chairs across from the first selectman's desk, and she stumbled a bit to keep her balance. She'd get him for that.

"That's right." Kayleigh stood behind Liam's chair, deliberately looming over him like vulture Snoopy. "The fireworks display."

"Well, then, this will be a quick meeting, because like I told you on the phone, we're cancelling the display this year."

"And like I told you on the phone, there's no need." Kayleigh pulled out the printout from the website she found that was selling discount fireworks. "I just need Liam to sign off on this company coming to town. They're willing to deliver on July third, and get full payment of twenty-five thousand dollars upon delivery. We don't have to worry about a deposit, and as long as Liam thinks they're on the up-and-up, we're good to go."

Liam took the paper she offered him and glanced it over. "Seems sketchy."

That was her first impression, too, but she had hoped she was wrong.

"I've officially taken the fireworks display off the agenda," Evan said.

"Put it back on, then." Kayleigh crossed her arms in front of her chest.

"The money would be better spent on other things."

"Perhaps, but the budget was voted on and approved with this money going toward fireworks. You can't spend it on something else without a special vote and no one wants to get into that."

Evan made a face. "Of course not, but it would look really good to come in with a fifty-thousand-dollar surplus at the end of the year."

"No, it won't,' she said. "That will give the town fuel to cut our budgets by fifty-thousand dollars next year because we didn't spend it."

"Or we could just hold it in trust for next year's fireworks," Evan said.

"I'll do a background check on this company if you want, Evan," Liam said. "But I don't want to waste my staff's time if you've already decided."

"No fireworks," Evan said. "Is that all?"

"No, it's not all," Kayleigh said, keeping her temper in check. "I want to know why you're shutting it down. It's like you were just waiting for an excuse."

"Kayleigh, it's just not that big a draw anymore. Kids and their parents have better things to do. If they want to watch fireworks, they'll watch them on television in the comfort of their own homes."

"That's kind of the point, Evan. The summer festival is a place for families to come together. It's the last weekend before the tourists descend on us. The town has always gathered for that last moment of sanity until we're on the express train to Labor Day."

"They're already flooding in," Liam said grumpily.

Mulberry had always been a not-so-secret summer getaway. It was close enough to New York City, without the skyrocketing prices of rent and goods. And it was on the water and an easy drive from anywhere in New England. Coupled with their historic buildings from the seventeenth and eighteenth centuries, there was enough in Mulberry to keep a family entertained for a week or more of summer vacation. Most of the stores around the town green made their entire year's rent in the month of July.

"We're not cancelling the summer festival," Evan said. "Just the fireworks portion."

"But we don't have to," Kayleigh said.

"What do you think, Chief?" Evan asked.

Liam gave him a sour look. "I think you're throwing me under the bus here."

"I'm asking you why you don't want the fireworks show."

Kayleigh arched an eyebrow at him.

"It's one less thing to worry about. Things are already

crazy, without adding fireworks into the mix. We get called out for noise-violation complaints. Dogs go crazy, wildlife is displaced. Personally, I'm all for a nice quiet Fourth of July."

"I agree," Evan said.

"In fact, I wouldn't mind if you cancelled the whole darn week."

"I disagree," Evan said.

"That's because all you do is stand up and wave during the parade at the end of the week."

"What the heck happened to you two fuddy-duddies?" Kayleigh asked. "Don't you remember how much fun we used to have at the end of the festival, how we would all pack our picnic coolers and chairs and sit out under the stars? Or go out on Mom's boat to watch." She had to stop because, for a horrifying moment, she thought her voice was going to crack. There was an uncomfortable silence and both men avoided looking at her. It gave her what she needed to rally. "You could feel the boom of the fireworks in your chest and get lost in the dazzling colors. Then, and only then, did summer officially start."

Evan smiled nostalgically. "I remember. But nowadays, there's too much to do and too much to arrange to get this squeezed in at the last minute."

"That's why I'm willing to take control over the fire-works portion. Like my mother did."

The sudden silence was shocking.

She hadn't meant to say that. She knew both men had loved her mother very much. Kayleigh didn't want this to be emotional blackmail.

Evan pointed at Liam. "You'll . . . you'll need his help too. He's got to sign off on the delivery and assign a detail to it."

"You'll help me, right?" Kayleigh turned to Liam, but wasn't encouraged by what she saw in his face.

"No. It's a pain in the neck to run around investigating every incident where some yahoo sets off a bottle rocket as a possible 'shots fired.'"

"Is this really about Chris Danvers hurting himself last year with the M-80?" she asked, turning to Evan.

He sighed. "The optics on fireworks aren't good because of that tragic incident. So yes, it has played a part in my decision."

"I think by not having the fireworks display, we're running the risk of it happening again."

"I disagree," Liam said. "I think the incident is still fresh enough in everyone's minds that there won't be a repeat."

"Can't you see that the kids who want the fireworks will find a way to put on their own show?" Kayleigh said.

"People can go buy all the legal fireworks they want, and as long as they're done by ten p.m., it's not a noise violation. If they get any of the aerial ones, those are illegal, and we will prosecute. We'll be making special rounds to make sure we avoid another incident like last year as well."

"You're going to arrest kids?" Evan frowned.

Kayleigh hid a smile as Evan's political nightmare radar went off.

"For their own safety, we will certainly confiscate the fireworks, but we're not going to haul anyone into the station in cuffs. I imagine there will be fines or community service handed out, though."

"That's a negative way to start off the summer," Evan said.

"I uphold the laws. If people decide to break them, then they face the consequences," Liam said, sounding defensive.

This was getting out of hand. "Most of this could all be avoided by giving them the safe, expected fireworks show that we've always done in the past," Kayleigh said. "It's tradition."

"People are just going to have to get used to a new tradition," Liam said.

"No, they don't," Kayleigh said between her teeth. She wished everything wasn't so cut-and-dried with him.

"Look," Evan said. "I could listen to you two bicker all day. It never gets old. But the fact of the matter is, I agree with Liam. The fireworks show is a nuisance. It's expensive, and it's a luxury item. The town really should have put the money toward other things."

"Perhaps, but the budget was voted on and approved. We've lost twenty-five thousand of that until the insurance kicks in, but we still have the other half to buy fireworks."

"From a company that, on the surface, doesn't seem legit," Liam said.

"If it is, will you support me on this?"

"It's not my decision to make. It's Evan's." Liam pointed at him.

"If I can pull this together, and show you that this is what the town wants, will you put the fireworks back on the festival's agenda?" Kayleigh challenged Evan.

"I'm not going to make any promises—"

"Spoken like a true politician," Liam interrupted.

"But if you can show me that Mulberry wants the show to go on," Evan said, counting on his fingers, "and if you can make the arrangements without taking away from the police chief's or your department's duties—and if you can get Liam on board with the idea—I'll reconsider my decision."

"I can't believe you're making me the bad guy in this," Liam said to Evan.

"Wow, look at those tread marks from the bus he just threw you under." Kayleigh slapped her hands on Liam's shoulders. "Come on, Liam, we've got work to do."

"What do you mean 'we'?" Liam stood and came around the chair to face her. "You heard Evan. This is your project, not mine."

Kayleigh refused to back away and they were thrillingly too close to each other. "You're being stubborn and unreasonable."

"Pot, kettle."

Evan clapped his hands to get their attention. "I don't care where you take the argument, just get out of my office. You don't have to go home, but you can't stay here." Evan made shooing motions with his hands. "I've got a meeting with the inland wetlands committee to find out if there's a way that we can shore up some of our sea-level areas so that we don't have to worry about having to deal with what Triumph Fireworks just went through."

With a last glare at Evan, Kayleigh left the first selectman's office. She had to hurry after Liam to catch up with him.

"The kids are really going to be disappointed if we cancel."

He shrugged. "They'll get over it."

She jerked on his arm to get him to stop walking. "When did you become such a sourpuss?"

"When I became police chief and had to deal with all the nonsense that comes with events like this."

"Don't you remember when we were their age? We used to go to the fair, and at the end, we'd sit down on the beach and watch the fireworks explode above us." She deliberately didn't mention the kiss.

"Yeah, I remember," he said. "And I remember we always got a couple of little ones to set off ourselves from your cousin Bobby. And we would light them up after everybody went home. It's a miracle one of us didn't end up like Chris Danvers."

"Well, yeah," she said. "I'm trying to avoid situations like that nowadays."

"I'm just saying. Kids are going to set off fireworks whether we have a big display or not. It's more work for my department and I'm busy enough as it is."

"Maybe you should take some time off?" she suggested. Could she maybe parlay this into asking him out for a date?

"Why? So you can try to steamroll over Ada?" Ada Gomez was his deputy chief.

So much for the date idea.

"I'd like to see anyone try to steamroll over Ada."

Kayleigh snorted. "Just do me a favor and keep an open mind. I'm going to prove to you and Evan that the town cares about the fireworks."

"I wish you luck," Liam said, holding out his hand.

She shook his hand, and as usual, his firm grip and the hard calluses on his palm made her think of naughty things. Kayleigh held on to her sigh as he released her hand and walked away. He had no idea that she still had the world's biggest crush on him.

Chapter Six

L IAM SIGHED. SHE had no idea that he still had the world's biggest crush on her. It would have been so easy if he could have just agreed with her about the fireworks, but that wasn't his way. If he could have found it in him to bend, they could have bonded over this. Instead, he headed back to his desk and tried not to think about all the ways he could have asked her out.

After doing some paperwork, Liam decided to take a walk around the town green to do his own research about who wanted fireworks, and who didn't, in this town. Because he knew if Kayleigh was the only one talking to people, she might be tempted to slant things her way.

The town workers were setting up a makeshift stage in the center of the green for the annual Shakespeare offering from the New Haven Shakespeare Society. This Sunday, they were putting on the play *Much Ado About Nothing*, which summed up Liam's opinion of the fireworks controversy.

While he walked around the green, he scanned the crowd. He could see that some of his officers were busy helping the town. One was directing traffic, another was writing a ticket out for jaywalking, and another was helping a kid with his bicycle. Looked like a flat tire.

He noticed Phyllis Moore walking his way with Quinn, her enormous husky.

"Chief, can I talk to you for a minute?"

"Sure, what can I do for you, Mrs. Moore?"

"Call me Phyllis. I want to report that Suki Meyer is not picking up after her dog." She shook a green plastic bag at him menacingly.

Liam took a step back and hoped he wouldn't have to dodge anything that came flying out of it. "I'll make sure to have the officers pay more attention."

"I appreciate that, Chief."

"Say, Mrs. Moore—I mean, Phyllis—have you heard about the first selectman canceling the fireworks show on the last night of the summer festival?"

"Yes. I'm glad. Quinn gets so afraid. I have to put a ThunderShirt on him, and he still cowers and whines until the show is over."

Liam hid a smug smile. Phyllis Moore was Kayleigh's neighbor. If she wouldn't listen to Liam, maybe she would listen to her neighbor. When Johanna died, Phyllis had taken over, acting like a surrogate mother for Kayleigh and her sisters. Kayleigh doted on her, always checking in and bringing her dinner now and then.

Liam stopped into the coffee shop for an iced latte. While he was waiting for the owner to finish up the order he was working on, Liam rested his hip on the high stool by the coffee bar and shamelessly eavesdropped on the conversations around him. For the most part, it was just small-town gossip and good-natured bickering. People were talking about entering their livestock in the summer fair. Some were complaining about the traffic and the lack of parking spots in town because of the tourists coming in.

He picked up the program for the summer festival and saw that it was packed full of activities for the entire week. On opening day, the town officials were judging the livestock and arts and crafts, and at night there were a bunch of musical acts coming in. Tuesday was the chili contest. Liam felt that this was their year, the one where they'd beat the firefighters. Throughout the week, there would be midway games, carnival rides, and everything from a petting zoo to high-wire trapeze acts. It was going to be an exhausting stint for his department. Not having the fireworks show at the end of it meant he could give his crew a break.

After Liam paid for his drink and was walking out the door, he wasn't surprised to run into his mother. Small town. Small world.

"Liam, I heard you and Kayleigh had a fight today."

Liam winced as several heads swiveled in their direction. "No, Mom. We had a minor difference of opinion."

"About what?"

"I need to get back to work. We can talk about this later."

"If it's not that big a deal, you can tell me on the way back to your office." She followed him outside.

"Weren't you just about to get something to drink?"

She took the latte out of his hand and took a sip. "This will do."

Signing defeat, Liam walked with his mother back to his office. "What do you think about not having fireworks this year?"

"I think it's ridiculous not to have them. We've had a show every year. So what if we're not going to have the full display? Even a shorter program is better than none at all."

"At this point," Liam said, "we don't even know if we can get the fireworks."

"You canceled the show without even trying?" His mother took another long drink of his latte and then waggled the cup at him. He took it back and sipped on the drink before answering her.

"Kayleigh is looking into it. But I think we're better off skipping this year because of what happened to Chris Danvers last year."

"So the entire town has to suffer because of a little boy's foolishness?"

"Of course not. I just didn't think the fireworks were that important anymore."

"Traditions are always important," his mother said. "A lot of things that we used to do in this town have faded away. I remember when we would get the day off from school on the first day of the summer festival. Now, summer festival doesn't start until the week before Fourth of July when school is already out. It's still a fun festival, but it was a lot more fun when we were allowed to play hooky from school." She put her hand on his arm. "You've been working really hard. You should take some time off. You're becoming an old man."

Ouch.

No one tells you the truth like your mother. Liam did feel like an old man sometimes. It seemed the best years of his life had passed him by, and he had settled into boring adulthood.

"Have you asked your mystery woman out to dinner yet?"

"Mother," he said, drawing the name out three or four syllables. "I don't need any help getting a date."

"That's not what it looks like from where I'm standing. Neither one of us is getting any younger. And I need some grandbabies." She made grabby hands at a toddler in a carriage far off in the distance.

"You're scaring me. You really are."

"Have you called Irene Mulberry?"

"No, and I'm not going to."

"What's wrong with her? You have so much in common."

Yeah, like an address in the Hills. "I'm looking to date a girl from the Harbor."

Lila sucked in a breath and her mouth puckered, as if she had been drinking tart lemonade instead of his latte. "Do you think that's a good idea?"

"I do."

"How do you know she's not just after your inheritance?"

"Because she couldn't care less about things like that."

"Don't be naive, Liam. Who is she?"

"Why? So you can scare her off? No. I'll tell you when

I'm ready." If he ever got ready.

Lila sighed in exasperation. "Do something about your social life, sooner rather than later. And I want you to work with Kayleigh, rather than work against her. She's a war hero, and if she wants fireworks on the Fourth of July, she should get them."

Liam hated it when his mother had a point. And now he could add feeling guilty to being disappointed in himself for not seeing eye to eye with Kayleigh.

THE POLICE SCANNER on his coffee table went off just as Liam was dropping off into a light doze. Ironically, Firemen's Field, a rental property where private events were held, was on fire. Scrambling up from the couch, Liam stepped back into his shoes. He grabbed his keys and headed out to his squad car. They certainly didn't need him. He wasn't on duty, but the thought that he might see Kayleigh was a lot more enticing than staying on his couch with one eye open, binge-watching a Netflix series that he had no real interest in.

He heard the sirens in the distance, so he flicked his lights on and sped up. When he arrived, he parked on the side of the road and walked down to the field just as the fire crew was putting out the last of the flames. There was a heavy veil of smoke in the air. Liam coughed and wrinkled his nose at the smell of burning hay and wood.

Liam walked up to Kayleigh, who was leaning against the

truck in full gear, minus the helmet. "So, what do we have here, Chief?"

She looked up at the sky as if seeking strength, and muttered something unintelligible.

Liam tried to translate it. "Did you just say bottle rocket?"

"Yes." She sighed loudly.

He would not smile. He would, though, put his hands in his pockets and rock back and forth on his heels. "You don't say?"

"Do you have to gloat?"

"I thought everything would still be too wet to catch fire from a stray spark."

"Yeah, so did your two teenage delinquents." She pointed over to the gazebo where the kids sat. "Go easy on them. They could have run or made the call anonymously. Instead, they called it in on their phone and waited here for us to arrive."

Liam saw that they were with one of his officers, so he stayed by Kayleigh's side. "At least no one was hurt. How did the fire start?"

"From what I understand, they had a series of ten rockets propped up in the ground and in a line. They ran down the line, lighting each one on the way. Most of them went up in the sky as normal."

"I hate that earsplitting whistle they make."

She rolled her eyes. "One of them fell flat because it wasn't in the ground tight enough. It flew parallel to the ground and hit the hay bale. When it exploded, the hay went up in flames and then started to spread. We were lucky we had all that rain last week."

There was another awkward pause as Liam tried to come up with something that wouldn't sound forced. With Kayleigh, he never knew what to say, so he said nothing.

"I can feel you straining not to say I told you so," she grumbled. "But it just proves my point. There are going to be a lot more of these on the Fourth if we don't have our fireworks show."

"I don't want to talk about fireworks," he said.

"Then why are you here?" Kayleigh glared at him.

That was so encouraging. Not. But then he thought back to his mother's words about tradition and having fun. "I heard that Checkers has s'mores ice cream tonight."

She cocked her head at him. "They're on summer hours now, right?"

"Open to eleven," he confirmed.

"Let me finish up here and I'll meet you there."

Liam nodded, keeping his cool until he got back to the squad car. Then he allowed himself a quiet "Yes!" and a fist bump on his dash that accidently pinged dispatch.

"Yeah, Chief?" the tinny voice said.

"Uh . . . radio check."

"Loud and clear, boss."

He started the car, hoping no one saw him do that, and drove to Checkers.

About a half hour later, Kayleigh showed up. Only she brought the entire crew, everyone who was at the fire, but wasn't on duty, with her. Liam probably should have been more specific. But he joined the group, helping to line up all the small, rectangular tables so they could sit together.

"Here," Kayleigh said, handing him a vanilla soft-serve cone dipped in rainbow sprinkles.

"That's festive," he said. "It's like fireworks."

"I knew you'd see the symbolism in that."

Liam shrugged. Ice cream was ice cream, and covering it with little candy pieces made it even better.

She slid into the chair next to him. Everyone else had cones, but she had two scoops of the s'mores ice cream, smothered in marshmallow and chocolate topping, with graham cracker crumbs and a dollop of whipped cream. She would have had a cherry on top, but when she got up to get some napkins, he stole it from her.

"She's going to kill you," Hank said.

"Bring it," Liam said, unconcerned. "So, where do you guys stand with the fireworks display?"

"With the chief," Cooper Pierce, one of the new trainees, said.

"I'm going to miss it," Ricki Carson, a veteran of the squad, said. "It's a lot of fun, both behind the scenes and watching it."

"To heck with that," Paul Mulberry said. "I'm looking forward to the police-officers-versus-firefighters chili cook-off. You'll see fireworks all right, when you taste the special sauce I've got cooked up."

Paul was Irene's brother-in-law. He had just been texting a bunch of things to someone. Liam worried that he had invited Irene, to join them for ice cream. According to

Liam's mother, Irene was a widower and very much looking for a new Mr. Mulberry. Rubbing his face, Liam stifled a groan. His mother was making him paranoid. Not everyone was a matchmaker.

"Chili in July just seems silly," Pam Stewart, another firefighter, said. "It should be an ice-cream-eating contest." She waved around her cone.

"Think of the mess." Paul sneered. "So, are you coppers ready to lose?" he asked Liam.

"Ada found her secret recipe from her grandmother down in Guadalajara, so don't get cocky."

"It's got ghost peppers in it, doesn't it?"

"I couldn't tell you," Liam said.

"You're a jerk," Kayleigh said, after she sat down and saw that her sundae was missing a cherry. She slugged him in the arm.

"Ow, why do you think I did it?" he asked. "It could have been Hank."

"He did it," Hank said, jerking his thumb at Liam.

"I know he did it. He's been doing it for the past twenty years."

While Liam would have liked this to have just been the two of them, he didn't mind hanging out with the fire crew. And he knew if he waited long enough, they would fade off to either go back home to their families or out to a restaurant or bar. If Kayleigh decided she wanted to continue their conversation at the Mulberry Tavern, he couldn't decide if he was going to tag along or make a dignified retreat.

"So, is it true that the two of you and Selectman Johnson

all grew up here in Mulberry?" Cooper asked.

Kayleigh looked at Liam and smiled. "Yup. Kindergarten through high school."

"That's really cool," Ricki said. "I don't keep in touch with anyone from high school anymore."

"We moved around a lot," Pam said. "So I know what that's like."

"I was a few years ahead of them," Paul said.

"Paul led the football team against our rivals, the Maddington Tigers, for the four years he was the quarterback," Liam said.

"Those were the days," Paul said. "What was your game in school?"

"Hockey," Kayleigh and Liam said at the same time.

"My mom drove us to the rink at four thirty a.m. every day for practice," Kayleigh said.

"She was a saint," Liam said and put his hand on hers. But it was sticky and they both scrambled for napkins to clean up.

Smooth. Real smooth.

"Liam was the best goalie I'd ever seen," Kayleigh said. "Coach Branson said he could have been an Olympian."

Liam wished he had his cone left to concentrate on. Instead he forced a neutral expression on his face and said, "I'm sure he was being kind."

"No," Paul said. "I remember. You were hot stuff in the creche. Nothing got by you."

"Thanks. Those were the days," he repeated, and lifted his water glass in a toast, hoping he wouldn't choke on the water.

He had wanted to try out for the Junior Olympics, but his parents hadn't wanted any part of it. They didn't want to drive him to practice, or pay for the equipment or the national meets. Kayleigh had wanted to qualify as well, but her parents had talked her out of it. Looking back, he could understand that money had been tight. He wished he could have loaned her the money or helped her with scholarships. But even if she'd have accepted it, her parents would never have allowed it. Still, Liam should have tried harder. Johanna would have driven them to the meets and Liam and Kayleigh could have gotten closer—as teammates, and maybe, something more.

Too distracted by his brooding, Liam didn't notice Irene had come in until she plopped down into the seat next to him.

"Liam, what a pleasant surprise." She leaned in and kissed him on the cheek.

"Yes," he forced out, trying not to jump up in shock.

"Well, that's enough sugar for me." Kayleigh stuffed the napkins in her empty sundae cup. The scraping back of her chair sounded loud to his ears. "I'll see you at the softball game, Chief," she said with a heavy clap on his shoulder.

Liam guessed it was too much to hope for that he would get a kiss on the cheek from Kayleigh. Still, his shoulder felt warm and tingly from where she'd swatted him.

Chapter Seven

KAYLEIGH WALKED ONTO the softball field with Leah and Samantha. Leah had her bat over her shoulder and her baseball hat on backward. Samantha wore mirrored sunglasses. She said she did it to keep the sun out of her eyes, but Kayleigh knew it was because she thought she looked glamorous. Today was the wildly anticipated police-officers-versus-firefighters game. The police historically won, leaving the firefighters to buy the beer for the after-game party. Kayleigh was just glad she had found her softball uniform. It had been thrown in the back of the closet since last year. Thankfully, she had washed it first.

"Why didn't you tell me that Irene Mulberry and Liam MacAvoy were dating?" Kayleigh asked them.

Samantha almost dropped her baseball glove that she had been throwing up and down. "What are you talking about?"

"That's ridiculous," Leah said. "She's about ten years older than him."

"That doesn't mean anything," Kayleigh said.

"No, but she's got a daughter who's going to graduate high school next year," Leah said. "She's going to be Miss Mulberry for the parade next Sunday."

"What makes you think they're dating?" Samantha

asked.

"She kissed him on the cheek last night at Checkers."

"That doesn't mean anything," Leah said.

As they walked into the dugout, they looked out to the stands, and sure enough, Irene Mulberry and her daughter, Karla, were sitting in the bleachers on the police side. Jules was sitting with them, the traitor.

"Dad!" Leah waved her hands to get his attention. "Wrong side." She pointed to where the firefighter cheering section was.

"Smile, Leah." Jules pointed his phone at her.

"Don't you dare make that gesture." Kayleigh grabbed Leah's hand down.

"Sam, you get in the picture too," Jules called over.

"Yeah, get in here." Leah dragged her sister in and they made faces at their father.

"You know this is going on Facebook, right?" Samantha sighed.

"Yeah, maybe it will go viral." Leah squirmed away.

"What are you going to do if Liam is dating Irene?" Samantha said.

"The same thing I've been doing for the past year," Kayleigh said. "Nothing. If Liam was interested, he would've made his move long before now."

"Why haven't you made your move?" Leah asked.

"Yes. Take the bull by the horns and ask him to go to the movies or something." Samantha grabbed the clipboard to fill out the roster.

"I could," Kayleigh said. "But he'd probably think I was

asking just as friends."

"Well, plant one on him in front of God and everybody." Leah adjusted her shin pads and slammed her fist into her glove. "He'll get the hint."

"Yeah, because that worked out so well for us last time," Kayleigh said.

"Oh, for Pete's sake, you were kids. No one cares anymore."

"I care. I don't want to make it awkward."

"It would only be awkward for a minute," Samantha said. "He'll probably turn bright red, stammer a few words, and then pretend that it never happened."

"Ouch," Leah said. "But Sam's right. It's been a long time. You've probably been friend-zoned."

"Yeah," Kayleigh sighed. "Friend-zoned."

Kayleigh dropped the subject as the rest of the team filtered into the dugout. She helped Leah warm up her pitching arm on the field until Ricki, their catcher, suited up. Samantha and Leah weren't firefighters, but since they were her sisters and the firefighters were short players, nobody really cared. Besides, if push came to shove, Leah had been an EMT at one point and, if the police wanted their cars fixed by Samantha, they knew better than to complain.

Ricki replaced her behind the plate and Kayleigh walked over to Samantha, who was stretching.

"Enough about my love life, or lack thereof," Kayleigh said. "What's the deal between you and Evan? You went out on a few dates and then . . . crickets."

Sam rolled her eyes. "Even if I did plant one on Evan, I

still think he'd be like, 'What was that for?' Or more likely, 'Don't do that. Your sister might see,' as if you'd beat him up or something because we were out on a date."

"Do you want me to have a talk with him?"

"No, of course I don't you to talk with him. That's embarrassing. We're both adults. If we can't work it out between ourselves, it wasn't meant to be."

"It was so much easier in kindergarten. I should have gotten you to pass a note to Liam saying 'If you like Kayleigh, check A for yes, B for no.'"

"We can still do that." Leah said, walking up to them. "Sometimes that's what it takes."

"Yeah, like you're the expert," Samantha said. "Who are you dating?"

"I've got my eye on a few people. I just haven't decided on whose life I want to grace with my presence."

"That's a good attitude," Kayleigh said, but she saw Leah's eyes linger on Hank for a beat too long.

Interesting. If both her sisters settled down with Hank and Evan, that would be a great reason to stay in town. The fireworks display this year would serve two purposes—it would be a memorial to her mother and an apology for missing her funeral, but it could also be a symbol of her emerging from the shell of protection she had wrapped herself in since her mother had passed.

With the final explosion of color, Kayleigh could be free of all the guilt and pain she'd carried around for too long.

It was something to think about.

Once everyone was in position on the field, they had a

half hour to practice. Kayleigh hit some balls to the outfield and then did some infield practice. Once the police team got there, they yielded the field.

Back in the dugout, Kayleigh nonchalantly glanced over to see what Liam and Irene were up to.

"Is he just clueless with all women, or is he really not into Irene?" Leah asked, leaning up on the chain-link fence, making no attempt to hide that she was staring openly at Irene and Liam.

"I think that's just how he treats women, with awkward indifference," Samantha said.

"I think it's sweet," Kayleigh said. "He's not swaggering or posturing or any of that toxic masculinity baloney. He's a solid friend and there's not a lot of nonsense with him."

"There's not a lot of anything with him," Leah said. "He just walked right by Irene with only a casual wave."

"Hey, Kayleigh," Liam said, coming over to the dugout.

"Oh," Leah said, drawing out the word. "Kayleigh gets a smile."

"Shut up," Kayleigh muttered under her breath. "Don't make it weird."

Liam threw the ball into his glove. "So, how many Baker sisters am I going to strike out today?"

"Them's fighting words," Kayleigh said.

"How about zero?" Samantha said.

"I'm going to run a line drive right between your eyes," Leah snarled.

Liam didn't even flinch. He was used to their reactions. "Then you'd be out when I catch it."

Evan, the umpire for the game, came over wearing a ratty old chest protector and a face mask on top of his head. "I need the rosters for both your teams."

Kayleigh grabbed the clipboard and came around the backdrop to hand it to him. Liam got his from Ada. Evan looked them over. "All right. Let's get things going."

"Can you make an announcement before the game that the after-party is at Leah's house? She made strawberry shortcake and blueberry cobbler, and she's serving it with vanilla ice cream for a red-white-and-blue effect."

"Will do," Evan said.

"People are looking forward to this game almost as much as the fireworks," Kayleigh said.

Liam groaned. "Not this again."

"I read the report on the bottle rocket fire the other night," Evan said. "Liam, I need you to have a couple more squad cars looking around for this type of thing. I don't want it to escalate, especially up in the north part of town where the farms are. At least in the downtown area, Kayleigh's crew can plug into the fire hydrants. If we get one up north, we'll have to haul out that tanker and I don't know if I trust that clunker to make it much longer."

"Nothing is wrong with the tanker—" Kayleigh started to say, but Liam interrupted her.

"That a complete overhaul of the engine wouldn't fix. That thing is louder than most of the school buses."

"She'll run and she'll get there on time," Kayleigh said. "If I didn't think she could make it to a fire, I wouldn't roll it out. I'd never put anyone's life at risk."

"I know," Evan said. "I'm just saying that perhaps there should be a vote to use the leftover twenty-five thousand dollars for our civic departments' budgets, as opposed to fireworks."

"A new truck costs at least four times that amount," Kayleigh said civilly. "What you do have is three mechanics—me, my sister, and my father—constantly checking it. And we're a bargain. You probably should keep us complacent—"

"Complacent," Liam snorted.

"—by giving me the go-ahead for the fireworks."

"I'll tell you what," Liam said. "If you guys win today, I'll research your shady fireworks company to make sure it's on the up-and-up."

"It's a deal," Kayleigh said.

"Now, wait a minute. If you guys lose, you have to forget about using them."

"Deal. If we lose, we won't purchase fireworks from that company."

"And," Liam said, "since you've got less than a week to find another dealer, and since the other firework warehouses in the area are out of stock, you'll accept that there's not going to be a show this year."

"Nice try. All you'll win is my agreement to pass on this vendor."

"It's a start," Liam said.

They shook hands. "You're going down," Kayleigh said.

"We'll see." Liam chuckled.

"Play ball!" Evan called.

The game started out with good-natured rivalry and cat-calling, but as the innings went on, the game became a little more serious. Grim determination set in.

Liam had a good arm. His underhand fastballs were high-speed and deadly accurate. Luckily, Kayleigh had been swinging at them for the past twenty years or so, and she had the timing down. The first couple times she was up, she hit some solid base hits. One time, though, she popped one up to center field. Ada ran back, caught it in the air, and Kayleigh was out.

The crowd loved the theatrics of seeing both sides play off against each other, but then it came down to their last bat. It was the top of the ninth. The score was tied when Kayleigh went up for her last at bat of the game. Unfortunately, the bases weren't loaded. But if they could score one run, and then get three quick outs on the other team, the firefighters would win the game for the first time in five years.

Kayleigh squared off and wagged her bat at Liam. For a moment, their gazes locked, and she saw something in his eyes that made her swing late.

"Get your head in the game," she told herself, stepping out of the batter's box. Tapping her bat on her cleats, she glared at Liam, who had a smirk on his face. When she stepped back up to the plate, she pointed her bat out toward left field.

"What? You're Babe Ruth now?" Liam joked.

"Line drive right to his teeth," Leah jeered.

"Bloodthirsty, isn't she?" Liam said.

"She still hasn't forgiven you for running over her sled." Of course, that was also twenty years ago, but Leah held a grudge.

"She should've put it away, instead of leaving it in the middle of the driveway."

That's what her mother had said, even though Liam had insisted on paying for it. Liam threw a wild pitch and Kayleigh had to stop herself from reaching for it.

"Plate's over here." She tapped it with her foot.

So, of course the next one was a strike.

"That's two . . ." Liam said.

The next pitch was perfect, and she swung big. It sailed over Liam's head and right toward Ada again. Kayleigh sprinted to first base and was halfway to second when the ball dropped and bounced. Kayleigh hit the base and dug in for third.

"Hold up!" Samantha screamed.

With a glance over her shoulder, Kayleigh saw that Ada had the ball in her hand and was intent on throwing it to the catcher.

"The heck I will," Kayleigh gritted out, rounding third and heading for home.

"Go, go!" Hank yelled.

"It's going to be close," Ricki said. "I can't watch."

Kayleigh saw the ball come in too high for the catcher to reach. She grinned fiercely. Home run, baby. Then suddenly, Liam was covering the plate, his glove out to catch the ball tossed at him from the catcher.

"Slide, slide!" Leah shouted.

Kayleigh told her body to slide in between Liam's legs. Her foot should hit the bag just as his glove swung down to tag her. However, her body had other ideas. Instead of leaning back, it decided to dive forward. Her frontward slide became more of an awkward tackle because instead of sliding between his legs, she took Liam down, and wound up sprawled on top of him. The ball rolled out of his glove, and Kayleigh climbed up him to tag the base.

"You okay?" she panted.

"Yeah," he groaned, and then they both froze as his hand landed on her backside.

She had to admit, it felt pretty good there. He made a great cushion too, and she couldn't bring herself to roll off him just yet. They were nose to nose again, and this time, it wasn't her imagination that there was something going on.

"Unnecessary roughness!" one of Liam's patrolmen called out.

"Standing in the baseline!" Hank shouted back.

Evan loomed over them. "Anybody need an ambulance? No? Then get up before I give you a warning for delay of game."

"This isn't football," Kayleigh muttered, and rolled to her feet.

"Yeah?" Evan pushed his mask up. "Sure looked like you sacked the quarterback on that play."

She held out her hand to Liam, but he waved it away and stood up on his own. "I wasn't a quarterback and that was the lamest tackle I've ever had."

"You want another one?" Kayleigh said, stepping in.

"And if I did?" Liam squared off against her.

Wait. Were they talking about the same thing?

"Now, now, girls, don't fight. You're both pretty." Evan shoved them apart. "Play ball!"

They played hard, but in the end, they couldn't hold the police team off, and Liam's teammates managed to eke out another two runs in the bottom of the ninth. Dusty, sweaty, and a little dejected, the fire team shook hands with their rivals and went to go get the beer.

Chapter Eight

KAYLEIGH PACKED UP her softball gear. She was so tired, she was considering just going straight home and falling asleep in a warm bubble bath.

"Cheer up," her friend Patty Martin, who was closing in on being nine months pregnant, said. "At the end of this is strawberry shortcake and blueberry cobbler."

Patty had never given up on Kayleigh. She had sent her care packages in Iraq, made sure she hunted down her addresses while Kayleigh roamed around, trying to find some peace after she had been discharged. Sometimes when Kayleigh was feeling raw or couldn't sleep at night, she would take out Patty's letters and read them. They were always full of Mulberry gossip, and Patty wrote so well that, if Kayleigh closed her eyes, it felt like she was back home. Ultimately, it was Patty who helped her make the decision to move back to Mulberry—and not just because she was a real estate agent and got her a killer deal on a house.

"Well, right now," Kayleigh said, "I need a shower over anything else."

"Yes, you do," Patty said. "I'll try not to eat all of the shortcake, but no promises. I'll meet you over at the party." She slid off the bleachers with a hand on her back.

"Are you all right?"

"It's the heat. And those aren't the most comfortable seats."

"You should have brought a lawn chair," Kayleigh said.

"Then I'd never be able to get up."

Patty was married to a submariner and his boat was out on patrol. Unless a miracle occurred, Tully wasn't going to make it back for the birth of his first child. Leah and Samantha joined Patty and helped her to her car. Kayleigh liked being part of a community that took care of each other. Maybe she would stay in Mulberry after all. It was comfortable here and she had missed spending time with her sisters. Kayleigh only wished she could shake the feeling of restlessness that made her want to run.

"That was a lot of fun. You guys played real hard." Liam laid a hand on her shoulder.

"Yeah, you guys too. I'm sorry I tackled you. I was supposed to be all 'slide DiMaggio, slide,' but apparently, it was more Lawrence Taylor."

"I shouldn't have been on the base line."

"So, no hard feelings?" Kayleigh said.

"Of course not. Although I think you cracked my rib when you landed on me." He rubbed his side teasingly.

Kayleigh yanked up his shirt. "Let me see. Is there a bruise?"

And then they had one of those awkward moments again. As she was touching his chest, she noticed that Liam had a six pack of muscles on his abdomen. Those hadn't been there when they had gone swimming as kids or when they kissed under the fireworks when they'd been fifteen. Tugging his shirt back down, Kayleigh prayed that he didn't see her flaming cheeks. And if he did, maybe he'd just assume she was overheated from the game, not because she liked what she saw.

"Speaking of six packs," she said.

"We weren't speaking of six packs," Liam countered.

Kayleigh wished the ground would just open up and swallow her whole. "It's our turn to buy the beer because we lost." She hoped that covered up her gaffe. "Do you have a preference for brand?"

"You know the guys—quantity over quality. Whatever's on sale should be fine." Liam shifted on his feet and looked away from her. "When you get to Leah's, I want to talk with you about something."

Kayleigh was dying to know what he wanted, but she was also very much aware that she needed a shower, so she said, "Sure. I'll catch up with you later," and beat a hasty retreat to her car.

"What was that all about?" Patty asked. She was already in her car with the air-conditioning on high, but she rolled down the window when she saw Kayleigh.

"What do you mean?"

"Looks like you were getting a little handsy with the police chief over there."

"You saw that? Did everyone see that?" Kayleigh looked around, hoping nobody was staring at her.

"I don't think anyone else was paying attention, but it looks like you're finally going after your childhood crush."

"I was," Kayleigh said, "before all this fireworks stuff came out. We're on opposite sides of the argument and I don't think it's the best time to start something."

"Sure looked like the right time from where I was sitting."

"Who knows?" Kayleigh shrugged. "He did say that he wanted to talk to me."

"Well, I expect all the details." Patty slid the window back up.

Throwing her softball gear in the back seat, Kayleigh got into her own car, and drove back home. As she was getting out of the car, her neighbor Phyllis called to her. Phyllis was pushing eighty, but acted like she was half her age—until she couldn't.

"Kayleigh, dear," she said. "Do you think you could help me out with Quinn?"

"What's going on?"

"He's dug a hole under his doghouse in the backyard. He's burrowed himself in and no amount of cajoling is getting him to come out. And the doghouse is too heavy for me to lift."

"I can help you out with that." Kayleigh walked into the backyard and saw that the Quinn had done a number on the area under his doghouse. She wasn't sure how he'd done it, but he'd managed to dig a hole large enough that he could lie in the shade underneath the doghouse.

"Do you think it's cooler there for him?" Phyllis asked, coming over to stand next to her.

"Cooler than being in the doghouse," Kayleigh said. "But

not as cool as being inside your house with the air-conditioning."

"He likes being outside. Don't you remember the last time it snowed? It was like ten degrees below zero and the fool was out there frolicking like a child."

"Yeah." Kayleigh grinned at the memory. "We had to convince him with snowballs to come inside." Kayleigh had thrown a snowball into the house, Quinn had chased it, and Phyllis had closed the door behind him.

"All right," Kayleigh said to Quinn. "Get in the house."

He greeted her with his growly bark, as if he was talking to her. Quinn was one of those few huskies who, when he vocalized, it sounded like he was saying, "I love you." Of course it was more like "Rye ruv rooooo," but everyone who heard it assumed he was saying, "I love you." So pretty much, the husky got away with murder. He was a beautiful dog with bright blue eyes and was smarter than half the people she knew. But in addition to being smart, he was also cunning. Kayleigh had a feeling that she couldn't just pick up the doghouse, because the eighty-pound dog would probably come out of his hole and jump inside it. And that would make her drop it. No, she had to be smart about this. Why wasn't there a squirrel around when you needed one? Quinn hated squirrels.

"Have you tried throwing his ball?"

"I've tried everything," Phyllis said. "I was about to put his food out on the porch. I thought that when he gets hungry enough, he'll come in. But then he'll be covered in dirt and mud and that hole will still be there."

"If you can get him inside, I can fill in the hole he made and then place his doghouse on top of it."

"Let's try that," she said.

It didn't work, because apparently dog food wasn't a big draw. But Kayleigh sitting on the porch eating a ham salad sandwich sure got his attention. He slithered out of his hole and then casually sauntered up to her, sitting down and looking at her as if he was saying, "I too enjoy a hearty ham salad sandwich." As soon as he was up on the porch, he decided he wanted to go chase his ball and maybe earn a crust or more of the sandwich.

Kayleigh tossed the ball into the house, and he went after it. She closed the door behind him. "You better go in and keep him occupied."

"I don't know what I would do without you, Kayleigh. Thank you."

"No problem. It breaks up the monotony. Most people call the fire department to get their cats out of the tree. I get to lure a husky out from under a doghouse."

It was another hour before Kayleigh finished shoveling in all the dirt back over Quinn's hole and dragging the doghouse over it. She didn't have any hope that this would stop him from doing it again, but at the very least, the yard didn't look all torn up. Realizing that she was super late, but unbearably filthy, Kayleigh didn't have any other choice but to take a long, hot shower.

And that meant that by the time she got to Leah's house, it was slim pickings. Patty was sitting at the table, guarding the last two pieces of strawberry shortcake. Nobody was going to argue with the pregnant lady for hoarding food.

"I'm hoping one of those is for me," Kayleigh said, sitting down.

Patty pushed one of the bowls closer to her.

In retrospect, Kayleigh probably should have gone straight to Leah's house and showered there because all the good stuff had already been taken. People were still drinking and milling around, but Liam was nowhere to be seen. Kayleigh gratefully dug into the strawberry shortcake that Patty had saved for her.

"Where were you?" Leah asked, sitting next to them.

"I was helping Phyllis with Quinn."

"That dog's a handful," Samantha said, also joining them at the picnic table.

"Yes, but she loves him."

"And he 'ruvs' her," Patty said, mimicking the husky's cute way of growling.

"Where's Dad?" Kayleigh asked.

"He went back home to upload his pictures. He got a great one of you on top of Liam."

Kayleigh closed her eyes and groaned. That was all she needed. "It's a good thing we're his only friends on social media."

The strawberries were tart and sweet and the homemade whipped cream was perfect. Still, she had never found out what Liam had wanted to talk to her about, and it was bugging her. "Did Liam leave already?" Kayleigh asked, trying to sound nonchalant.

"He showed up and left with Irene Mulberry," Patty

said. "She conveniently lent her car to her daughter and needed a ride home. And since Liam's house is right on the way . . ."

"Rats," Kayleigh said. "You ever get the feeling that sometimes you waited too long and things have passed you by?"

"No," Patty said. "You haven't waited too long and things haven't passed you by. The two of you just need to have your heads knocked together. You've been friends forever, but now it's time to see each other as something other than friends."

"How do I make Liam see me as a woman and not just one of the guys?"

"You might want to stop being so competitive with him."

"Not tackling him on the baseball field might be a good start," Samantha said.

"He was in my way. He put himself between me and home plate. He would have been absolutely insufferable if he'd tagged me out."

"This competition thing between the two of you is complicated foreplay. One of you is going to have to back off."

"Let him do it, then."

Patty rolled her eyes. "I'm sure if I had this conversation with him—"

"Don't you dare," Kayleigh said.

"This hypothetical conversation with him, he would say that you need to be the one to back off first."

"Well, that's not going to happen."

"If you want something to happen, you're going to have to make an effort."

"Like what?"

"Invite him over and make him a romantic dinner," Patty said.

"That's a fantastic idea. Unfortunately, you know I can't cook, and so does he. He'll think I'm trying to poison him."

"You can cook," Leah said. "You're just too impatient to follow a recipe. But Mom has some easier ones. Pick one of them and you'll be fine."

"Her chicken cacciatore one is pretty simple," Samantha said.

"It's a hearty meal too. Lots of meat over pasta," Patty added.

"If I wanted hearty, why couldn't I just throw a couple steaks on the grill and bake some potatoes? Leah can pull up her lobster pots and get me a few of those too."

"Don't count on it," Leah said. "I haven't been getting many lately."

"I wouldn't do the surf and turf route on the first date," Samantha said. "That's more for special occasions. This is a friendly first date, a get-to-know-you dinner."

"I know Liam," Kayleigh said. "We all grew up with him. What if I just do take-out Chinese?"

"Not a bad date night dinner," Patty said. "But that's for more established couples, where you don't really have to try anymore and you're just having dinner for the companionship."

"I am doing this for the companionship."

"Yes, but you are in each other's friend zone. You want to break out of that rut. I think a nice Italian dinner with some garlic bread—"

"I thought garlic was a no-no on dates," Kayleigh said. It had been a while since she had put herself out on the dating scene—almost two years, ever since she came back to Mulberry—but she remembered that much.

"If you're both eating it, it cancels itself out," Samantha said.

Kayleigh wasn't sure if she was kidding or not.

"Don't forget the wine. Serve the chicken cacciatore up with a bold pinot noir for the perfect first step to romance," Patty read off from her phone.

"Don't take wine advice from the pregnant lady," Leah said. "You don't serve red wine with chicken."

"You do if it's a red sauce," Samantha argued.

Kayleigh held her head in her hands. "This is way too complicated. I can't do this."

"Yes, you can. Who cares what kind of wine is served? It's wine. It'll help settle your nerves."

"How about beer or soda?" Kayleigh said.

"No," all three of them said together.

"What's wrong with that?"

"Nothing, as long as you're okay with burping during a romantic moment," Leah said.

"I'm not even sure if there's going to be a romantic moment." Kayleigh pushed herself up. "This is never going to work."

Her sisters pushed her back down in her seat.

"It's not as complicated as we're making it out to be," Samantha said. "Leah will help you with the shopping and I'll pick up the wine for you. All you have to do is invite Liam and cook the meal. Can you do that?"

"Sure," Kayleigh said. She hoped. What was the worst that could happen?

Chapter Nine

L IAM WAS SETTING up the dunking booth in the Mulberry Fairgrounds. It was going to be a lot of fun, but if the heat kept up, he was going to be knocking himself into the pool. Wiping the sweat off his brow with his sleeve, he sat back on his haunches and wondered if the booth was crooked.

"We're going to make bank on Fire Chief Baker alone with you sitting here," Bill Weeks, one of his officers, said.

"Nah, Kayleigh can't hit the side of a barn."

He saw Bill's gaze flick to something over his head.

"She's standing behind me, isn't she?"

"The side of a barn, huh? You better wear your swimming trunks." Kayleigh sounded more amused than angry.

"Thanks for the heads-up, Bill." Liam groaned, stretching to his feet.

Bill put his hammer down. "I just remembered . . . I've got to do something way over there."

When they were alone, Liam said, "What are you doing here?" *Smooth, Liam. Real smooth.*

"Working. We're setting up the tables for the chili competition. And we've got two food trucks lined up and ready to use if we need to make more chili. That way we don't have to rent commercial kitchen space and haul the batches here and there. You know, because our prize-winning chili will be in demand."

"Are you all set with the permits?"

"Yup. All we need are the chefs."

"I'll tell Ada."

Hello, awkward silence, my old friend. There had to be something he could do to avoid it. He picked up Bill's hammer and gave it to her. "Don't just stand there. Help me with this thing." That wasn't much better, but at least they were spending time together. The noise from their hammers kept him from having to make small talk.

Once they had the frame of the booth up, Kayleigh sat down and rummaged around in his cooler for a bottle of water. "You left Leah's party before I got there. What did you want to talk to me about?"

Liam joined her on the ground. "I wanted to tell you that I was going to do a background check on the company anyway."

"A bet is a bet," Kayleigh said. "You don't have to do that."

"Well, I did." It hadn't taken that long and truth be told, he wanted to see if the company was legit or not. "On paper, they might have looked good, but when I called them up and let them know I was the chief of police, suddenly I needed to talk to their manager. And the manager was conveniently on vacation."

"Figures," she said. "Thanks. I appreciate that you took the time out to check."

"What are you going to do now?"

"Keep looking."

"You've got a short window."

"I know," she said. "And even if I find a vendor, I still have to convince you and Evan. But that's the easy part."

"Ya think?" Liam snorted.

"You'll see reason . . . eventually, and Evan just has to be convinced it's in his best political interest." She finished up her water, crumpled the bottle, and then tossed it into a nearby recycling can. "What are you doing tonight?"

"Why?" Liam asked suspiciously.

"Because I asked you." Kayleigh got to her feet and stretched.

"Nothing, but I'm not going to drive to Pennsylvania to find some fireworks with you."

"That wasn't the plan. Although that's not a half-bad idea. Instead of putting a bulk order in at the warehouse, I could just buy a whole bunch of the shells myself at roadside stands. Do you think they'll take a town check?"

"Kayleigh, I was kidding. You have to know that's illegal." Liam jumped to his feet.

"I'm not setting them off. I'm bringing them back here to be set off legally."

"You make my eyes cross," he said. "You're not looking at a ticket and a slap on the wrist. You're looking at jail time for crossing state lines with them."

"Not if I have a permit."

"You don't. You want to know how I know you don't? Because I know everyone who has a federal permit in Mulberry."

"You're really getting steamed about this." She grinned. "This is fun. I'm just yanking your chain." Kayleigh leaned in. "Or am I?"

Liam held up a finger. "First of all, please don't tell me about a crime you're going to commit before you do it. Second of all, there are cops waiting by the stands out there to take your license plate number and call it in, so you'll get nabbed as soon as you cross the Delaware River."

She was staring at him intently.

"What?"

"I was waiting for number three and I'm fascinated by the vein that's throbbing in your temple."

"It's not—" He reached up. Sighed. "I hate you."

"That's the most fun I've had all week. Anyway, what I really wanted to ask you was if you want to come up to my house and have dinner with me tonight."

"Why?" he said suspiciously.

"Because it's soon dinnertime and people like to eat," she said between her teeth. "You know what? Never mind. Forget I asked." She turned around and stomped away.

Idiot! Liam almost tripped over his hammer in his rush to catch up with her. "I'd love to come for dinner. Can I bring something? What are we having?"

"My mom's chicken cacciatore."

"Oh, man, I haven't had that in forever."

"Yeah," Kayleigh said. She stopped and turned around with a smile that made him feel goofy.

"What's the occasion?" He smiled back at her and hoped

he didn't look like the idiot he thought he was being.

"I wanted to cook."

"Are you feeling all right?"

"You know, I can go ask Bill if *he* wants to have dinner with me."

Bill had been coming back to work on the booth, but upon hearing his name, turned on his heel and walked in the other direction.

"No. No," Liam said. "I'm not passing up a chance to taste your mom's chicken cacciatore again. I'll bring dessert."

Kayleigh looked surprised. "Okay. Well, how about six o'clock?"

"Sounds great."

As Kayleigh walked away, Liam stood there and watched until Bill nudged him.

"Are you okay there, boss?"

"Yeah, fine."

"What did the chief want?"

"To invite me to dinner."

"I didn't realize the two of you were dating."

"We're not dating. At least, I don't think we are. Do you think this is a date?" He stared at his deputy, not sure if he could believe it or not.

"Well, you should bring flowers, just in case."

"Good idea." Liam clapped him on the arm.

"If you are dating, it's expected, and if you're not, it's still a nice gesture."

"Brilliant. I'm going to order the flowers now."

"Just don't make it roses."

Liam stopped in his tracks. "Why not roses? All women like roses."

"They do, but there's a lot of baggage attached to roses."

"What kind of baggage? It's a pretty flower."

"Well, if you give her a red rose, it represents passion and love. You don't want to rush the red roses. Those are usually for special occasions, like if she's making steak and lobster."

"What if she's making her mom's chicken cacciatore?"

Bill looked at his phone. "White roses are for purity. Yellow roses are for friendship. Peach roses are for gratitude. Pink is admiration. Any of these working for you?"

All of them, and none of them. "Why don't I skip the roses? This is a lot more complicated than I thought. Is there a rule book for this?"

"No, everyone knows this."

"I didn't know it." He tried to think back on his last date. He hadn't brought flowers. Maybe that's why there hadn't been a second date. Liam hadn't had a lot of time for dating this past year. The job kept him busy and he really didn't want to be with anyone but Kayleigh. "I thought I would just go have dinner and chat."

"You could certainly do that. But you want to do this right, don't you?"

"Absolutely," Liam said.

"Okay, skip the roses," Bill said. "But don't go getting those grocery store flowers either."

"What's wrong with them? What message do they send?"

"That you're cheap."

Liam shrugged. "I am cheap."

"Maybe so, but you don't want that to be her first impression."

"First impression? We've known each other for decades. She knows I'm cheap."

"That's going to be a problem."

"How?"

"Women don't like cheap guys."

Liam was starting to get a headache. He rubbed his forehead with his thumb and forefinger. "So, I can't get her roses because they have baggage."

"That's right."

"And I can't get her daisies or drugstore flowers, because they're cheap."

"You got it, boss."

"So what do I get her?"

"What kind of flowers does she like?"

"I don't even know if she likes flowers."

"All women like flowers."

"Maybe I should be talking to Ada about this."

"That's a good idea."

"You're a big help," Liam said, then walked back to his squad car and called his deputy chief. "Ada, I need to ask you a silly question. What kind of flowers should I bring to dinner?"

"What kind of dinner are we talking about?"

"A homemade one."

"Well, if we're talking Irene Mulberry, I know she likes irises."

"What if we're not talking about Irene Mulberry?" He

kept his voice down.

"Well, that would depend on who we were talking about, boss."

Liam groaned. "Only you and Bill know right now, and I'd like you to keep it a secret until I can figure things out."

"All right," Ada drawled.

"Kayleigh Baker invited me over for dinner tonight."

"Did she? Is this just like a dinner between friends?"

"That's the problem. I don't know," he said. "If it's not, I want to make sure I don't blow it."

"So, if she thought of you as more than a friend, you'd be interested?

"Yes, but I don't know if she's thinking that way. She's making her mom's chicken cacciatore recipe. It could be just because her mom used to make it all the time for us kids, and she wanted to share it with me."

"How sweet," Ada said. "I bet that's what it is."

Liam's heart dropped. "You think?"

"How would I know?"

"But do you see my dilemma? I was going to bring roses."

"Oh, no sir, you can't do that."

"Yes, I know. I get it. Baggage. So what should I bring?"

"Why don't you bring the wine?"

"She's having me bring dessert. I don't want to bring dessert and wine."

"You can't go wrong with another bottle of wine."

"Really? There's is no baggage attached to getting red instead of white wine?"

"No."

"Can't I just get beer?"

"No. What kind of dessert were you going to get?" Ada asked.

"I hadn't thought that far ahead. I was caught up in the flower conundrum." This was so much more complicated that he had thought. He should have asked her to dinner first.

"You can always get cheesecake or if you want to do something a little bit fancy, a box of Italian pastries would fit in with the Italian theme of the night."

"That's a good idea," he said.

"And about the flowers, just go to Mulberry Florist and see what they recommend."

"All right. Thanks for your help, Ada."

"You're welcome."

He went back to the dunking booth. "Bill, I've got to go. I'll talk to you later."

"Good luck at the chief's tonight."

"Keep it down," Liam said. "I don't want the whole world knowing about it until I know if it's a friends-date or a date-date."

"You told Ada. The whole world is going to know."

"I'm asking both of you to keep this under your hats for now."

"There's no point in hiding it. The whole town is going to know you had dinner at her house by tomorrow morning. I won't say a word, but these things have a way of getting out. I don't think Irene is going to be very happy to hear about this."

"That's her problem. I've never given Irene any reason to think there was anything between us." Then Liam got back into his car and drove to the florist.

"I'LL BE RIGHT with you, Chief," the florist said. "I have to put the finishing touches on these corsages for the Buckler wedding."

"Take your time." Liam browsed up and down the big refrigerators. He saw a couple of the bright pink Gerber daisies in a bucket. Big daisies like this seemed like a safe flower. Although, he would have to ask the florist if daisies had baggage like the roses did.

Liam remembered that Kayleigh liked wildflowers. Pansies were her favorite, and daffodils. Her mother had constantly yelled at her daughters not to pick her flowers for her, because she'd rather enjoy seeing them outside where they lasted weeks, instead of wilting after a day or two inside.

Johanna Baker had always made such a big deal about the first daffodil of the season. There was always one poking its head up early, and Johanna had called it her "rogue daffy."

"What can I do for you, Chief?"

"I'm going to dinner tonight, and I want to give the hostess some flowers, but I don't know what to get." He pointed to the Gerber daisies. "Do you think those would work?"

"Sure," she said. "Carnations are always a good choice too."

Liam hated feeling indecisive, but he didn't want to mess this up by doing something clueless. "Do you have any daffodils?"

She shook her head. "Too late in the season. You're better off getting bulbs to plant in the fall, but that's not necessarily a good hostess gift. Unless she's into gardening?"

Liam chuckled. "No, she's the only person I know that's killed a spider plant."

The florist whistled. "That's some skill. How about tiger lilies?"

"No lilies," he said. "They remind her of funerals. Do you have any wildflowers?"

"No." She shook her head sadly. "I know. How about a bouquet of peonies?" She showed him a bucket of puffy large flowers.

"Do the colors mean anything weird?"

"Not that I know of. I can put together a nice bouquet for you with a few salmon-colored ones to offset the reds and pinks. They're a step up from carnations and have a lovely scent."

"Perfect," he sighed. He should have come here first. This was like hitting the easy button.

"Does she have a vase to put these in?"

Liam heard the sound of screeching brakes in his head. He should have known it was too good to be true. "I don't know."

"Flowers make a great gift, but you don't want the hostess searching around for a vase. I have a crystal-cut one here I can put them in. Or would you prefer a simple glass one?"

There was nothing simple about this. Nothing. "At this point," Liam said, handing her his credit card. "I just want this to end. Whatever you suggest is all right by me."

He still needed to order the Italian pastries. Liam hoped that there wasn't anything suggestive about cannoli and clam shells.

Chapter Ten

KAYLEIGH WASN'T GOOD in the kitchen under normal situations. But under pressure? That's when things got worse. She did well with the prep work, cutting the peppers and onions on her cutting board. She had browned the chicken thighs and legs on both sides and deglazed the pan with red wine, just like a fancy television chef.

She had all that simmering in a pot on the stove top and the garlic bread was toasting up in the oven. Setting the table, Kayleigh brought out a linen tablecloth and some fine china that she'd picked up at a yard sale. She lit two taper candles in candlesticks on the center of the table. Everything looked perfect. She was contemplating dipping into the wine when her phone rang. It was Phyllis.

"Kayleigh, I need your help with Quinn," she said.

"If he's under the doghouse again, he's going to have to stay there."

"No," Phyllis said. "It's worse."

"How could it be worse?" Kayleigh knew she was going to regret asking that.

"He's on the roof."

For a moment, Kayleigh thought she heard incorrectly. But then she pushed her lacy kitchen curtains aside and looked up. She couldn't see all of him, but there was definitely a wagging husky tail up there.

"How on earth did he get up there?"

"I left the upstairs window open, and he must have decided to jump out and investigate."

Craning her neck, Kayleigh saw that there was a narrow ledge that he could have used to jump from the window frame to the roof. It was a wonder he hadn't slipped and fallen to his death.

"Can you get him down?" Phyllis asked.

"I'm going to have to call this in. We can put him in a harness and lower him down to the ground. I think that will be safest."

"I hate to be a bother."

"No, this is a good training exercise," Kayleigh said. "I'll be over as soon as I send them out."

Then she called Hank, who was on duty at the firehouse. "I need to you send the ladder truck to my neighbor's yard. Quinn is stuck on the roof."

"Okay," Hank drawled.

"Bring someone that can deadlift a hundred pounds. Quinn's not that heavy, but he might start squirming around if we have to carry him down a ladder."

"This should be an interesting way to break up the day," Hank said. "We'll be there in a few."

"Thanks."

Kayleigh walked outside to get a better view of the situation. Sure enough, Quinn was lying down, basking in the sun, perfectly content to be lounging on an angled roof. She didn't want to call his name for fear that he might try to jump down and get hurt.

Phyllis joined her out in the yard and handed her a cup of coffee. "I never thought I'd have to keep my upstairs windows closed. Do you think he saw something and chased it?"

"Who knows with him? But if you can move your car either into the garage or park on the street, the firetruck can go right up to the house with the ladder."

"Okay," Phyllis said and moved her car into Kayleigh's driveway.

Within a few minutes, sirens wailing, the Mulberry Fire Department pulled up. Cooper expertly backed the ladder truck into the driveway, while Kayleigh kept a sharp eye on the lawn. The truck could really cut up the landscaping that Phyllis had worked so hard to keep perfect.

They sent the ladder up and secured it. Hank climbed up and when his torso was over the roof, he held out his hands for Quinn.

"Come on, boy," he said.

Quinn yawned at him.

"Don't make me come up there."

After a couple of minutes trying to coax him to come closer, Kayleigh threw Hank a tennis ball. "See if he'll come to you now."

"Do you want your ball, Quinn?"

Ears perking up, Quinn got down into the puppy-play pose, wagging his tail excitedly. His bark was more of a ruff that sounded like "yes."

"No, not on the roof. Hank, don't throw it. Just hold out your hand."

"That's what I'm going to do."

Quinn danced in place, his nails sliding on the roof tiles.

"Don't get him too excited," Kayleigh said.

"Do you want to do this?" Hank walked slowly backward down the ladder, holding the ball enticingly. "We need an aerial work platform on this thing."

"I know," she said. Her trucks needed a lot of things.

Quinn inched closer and came in range to sniff the ladder, but when Hank went to grab him, Quinn backed away, sliding down the side of the roof.

"Quinn," Kayleigh said, running out with her arms out, as if she might have to catch the falling dog. From that height, Quinn would probably crush her into the ground.

"That's it. I'm getting the harness. We're going to slip it on him and then lower him down with a rope."

She heard more sirens and the unmistakable loud chugging of the tanker truck. "Why the heck did you call in these guys for?"

"Slow day," Hank said. "They could use the practice and they're bringing the jump pad from the fairgrounds."

Sure enough, secured by bungee cords, a large inflated rectangle sat on top of the tanker.

"I don't believe what I'm seeing." Kayleigh watched as her team scrambled to take the bouncy pad down and carry it to the side of the house where Quinn was watching them and wagging his tail.

"I don't even think that's safe to use," Kayleigh said. Certainly, they would never have a human jump out of a burning building into it.

"It's a last resort in case he falls or jumps," Ricki said.

It should break his fall, but Kayleigh couldn't guarantee it was going to stop him from being hurt. Still, if Quinn did decide to jump, he wouldn't land on the ground. But he could break his legs or his back. Kayleigh didn't like how this could turn out.

"Phyllis, can you get me some of his treats?"

Armed with a handful, Kayleigh climbed up the ladder. She put a few treats at the top, and then one on every step of the ladder. She had his leash in her hand to clip it on just in case.

Quinn was more interested in all the people coming out to look at him.

"Darn it, Quinn." Kayleigh lost her patience and grabbed the harness from Hank. She hauled herself up the ladder and onto the roof. Staggering a little to keep her balance, she sat down and pulled out a dog biscuit. Quinn saw that she had it and cocked his head at her.

"If you want it, you're going to have to come here," she said.

Her plan was, once he got close enough, she would clip his leash on him and then wrangle him into the harness. If she couldn't lead him down the ladder, they'd try lowering him down via a rope. Or drag him to Hank and have him carry Quinn down. Hopefully, it wouldn't come to that, though.

"Glad to see that all my agility training with him paid

off," Phyllis said, squinting up at her.

"Yeah, too bad the obedience training didn't stick," Kayleigh replied. "Come on," she crooned at Quinn.

Inching closer to him, scooting along on her behind, she heard her smoke alarm go off.

"Oh, no! The garlic bread." Her kitchen curtains caught on fire. "Guys!" She pointed. "Kitchen fire. Stove top and oven!" she shouted down as the team on the ground scrambled.

"See," Hank said. "Training."

"Not funny," she called down. Kayleigh could smell the burning chicken from up here. She must have had the heat on too high or the sauce must have evaporated quicker than she thought. Dinner was ruined and her kitchen might be next.

Forgetting Quinn, she scuttled to the edge of the roof trying to see how bad is was. Her team used the tanker since it was on the street and rolled out the big hose. Ricki and Pam, in full gear, went into the kitchen first to access the situation. Kayleigh wished she had her radio on her. She knew, if it was safe to do so, they would shut off the stove.

Paul and Cooper rushed in with the hose and put out the drapes.

"This can't be happening." Kayleigh moaned. "What a mess."

"Better than having the house burn down," Hank said.

"At least no one was home."

She was never going to live this down. Never. But she supposed if you were going to have a house fire, having both trucks parked outside came in handy. It didn't take long for them to put out the fire. She got down flat on her belly so she could see into the kitchen. She coughed a little as the acrid smoke oil boiled out of the window.

"It smells like a grease fire, but I didn't have anything greasy in the oven. The bread is probably charcoal, but that shouldn't have done anything."

"The candles were knocked over," Hank said from the ground. "Caught the tablecloth on fire. Your table is ruined. The garlic bread saved you. The smoke from the oven set off your alarm. Not sure how the curtains got into it. Maybe the wind carried a spark."

"I can't believe I did that." She just wanted to lie on the roof and have a do-over. But first, she still had a job to do. "All right, Quinn. I have had enough of your nonsense." She stood up, but Quinn was nowhere to be seen. Rushing toward the ladder, she saw him safe and on the ground, sniffing around the truck.

"Phyllis," she called, dropping the leash to the ground. "He's down and he's okay."

She sank down on the roof in relief. She was glad he was okay, but she didn't want to face the mess in the kitchen.

"Are you going to come down?" Hank said. "Or do I have to haul you over my shoulder?"

"You're the one who wanted a training exercise," she said.

"I gave the all clear. You've got a mess on your hands, but the structure is undamaged."

"Leave the door open and air it out." This was awful.

Liam was going to be here any minute and there was no way the house would be ready for a romantic dinner, even if she could whip something up.

Of course, Liam chose that moment to drive up in the squad car. He pulled into her driveway and got out.

"You're early," she called down to him.

"I heard the dispatch call for the bouncy house and had to stop by and see if you needed assistance."

"Nope, as you can see. I've got everything under control."

"Why are you on the roof?" he asked. "Did you have to jump to flee the flames?"

"No. I had to rescue a dog."

Quinn brought his tennis ball to Liam, dragging Phyllis with him.

"How did that work out?"

"See for yourself." Kayleigh gestured to her house.

Her team was still stomping around, tidying up, winding up the hose, and resecuring the bouncy pad. Liam looked inside her house and then came back. "I'm going to go out a limb here, but I take it we're not going to have chicken cacciatore tonight."

"Nope," she said. "I was thinking of firing up the grill and having some burgers and hot dogs."

Her team cheered for that. Liam nodded. "I'll go pick up some beer."

The team cheered for that as well.

Kayleigh wondered how long she could stay on the roof. She might be able to live this down in a couple years. The roof was actually quite comfortable. She could see why

Quinn liked it. It was nice and warm on her backside and she had a great view of the neighborhood. Most of all, she didn't have to confront the mess in her kitchen.

After about ten minutes of self-pity, Kayleigh climbed down the ladder.

"Could have been worse, boss. You, of all people, should know better than to leave candles unattended and food cooking on the stove."

She held up her hand to stop any further admonishments. "If you really want to help, Hank, go into the garage and pull out the grill and get the coal started."

Kayleigh wasn't a stranger to house fires. And she had been on the other end of the hose, so she knew how lucky she was. Still, it was humiliating to have this happen. She'd been so distracted by dinner with Liam, it had come to this. Shaking her head, she sloshed to the freezer. Her sneakers and socks got soaked from the water pooling up on the floor.

Ignoring the soot stains on the ceiling and the reek of smoke, she pulled out five pounds of hot dogs and two boxes of premade burgers. She usually had that on hand for her team if they ever went back to her house after a fire and were hungry.

Kayleigh called Liam and he answered on the first ring.

"Don't tell me there are locusts or a plague at your house now?"

"Not yet, but the day isn't over. While you're out, can you pick up a couple dozen hot dog and hamburger buns? Dinner for two is now dinner for twelve."

"You got it, but I want a raincheck on the chicken."

"Me too," she said.

Chapter Eleven

I T WAS THE first day of the summer festival. The rides had been constructed by the amusement park rental company overnight while most of Mulberry slept. Liam had tried to outlast the firefighters last night, but they were fully entrenched as they discussed the repairs to Kayleigh's kitchen. He wound up being the first to go home out of self-preservation—he knew he was in for a rough week.

As much as he hated the level of security that was needed at the festival, Liam was a sucker for the fried dough and the homemade soda. So he walked around, stuffing his face and making himself sick on the bubbly, overly sugared drink. He felt like a kid again. Maybe Kayleigh had a point about the festival being fun if he could just relax and enjoy it. Looking at the program of events, he saw that today the selectmen were judging livestock, and the arts and crafts. Heading over to the pavilions, he was pleased to run into Kayleigh. She was judging the pies that had been submitted.

"How did you get such a sweet gig like that?" he asked, leaning against the chicken-wired booth.

"I told Evan that if he didn't choose me as a judge, I'd put a frog in his desk."

Liam smirked. "You wouldn't really have done that."

She pointed. "Emma James's chocolate cream pie. Mrs. Anginosta's cannoli cake. Brian Miller's lemon meringue pie."

"You don't have to rub it in. So who's the best?"

"They're all wonderful. I might just have to have a second taste."

Liam groaned. "Not fair. Next year I'm going to bring in a bucket of frogs." He watched her while she diligently took notes. "We missed Shakespeare on the green last night."

"I had enough drama going on, thank you very much," she said.

"Were you able to get a contractor to come in right away?"

"More or less. It's a good thing I eat most of my meals at the station."

Now was his chance. "What are you doing tonight?" he asked. They could go out for a nice, quiet dinner. No huskies, no firefighters, just the two of them. He was picturing driving up a few towns and getting Mexican food from an award-winning restaurant Ada recommended. Tomorrow his body would punish him for what he was eating today, but he was determined to live in the moment.

"Are you kidding me? Winston Jones is playing on center stage tonight. I'm going to be dancing my brains out."

Well, if that wasn't a kick in the gut.

"We were really lucky to get him."

"I hadn't had a chance to take a look and see what acts the summer festival committee brought in," Liam said, twirling his empty stainless-steel mug. He really wanted another birch beer, but the sugar was making him jittery.

"Were you living under a rock?" She cocked her head at him.

"Just been busy. There've been more break-ins lately. Mostly unlocked cars, but some of the houses by the highway have been getting hit too."

"What happened to the guy you arrested?" she asked.

"He was working alone, or so he says. Because the neighborhoods they're hitting are close to the highway, they have an easy escape. It's been difficult to track them. Mrs. Murray came home and found her screen door ripped off the hinges. Her jewelry was taken, along with some cash. You know what she said to me?"

Kayleigh shook her head.

"'But I locked my door.'" Liam rolled his eyes.

"At least no one was hurt."

"Not yet," he said. "I'm afraid that if we don't figure out a way to stop them, these thieves will get more brazen."

"Do you think it's more than one person?"

Nodding, Liam said, "I think so. The camera footage we've been able to get doesn't show us much. They're wearing hoodies. But there was one big guy, one medium-size guy, and I'm pretty sure a woman."

"Maybe you'll get lucky and get a license plate number off a street camera."

"We haven't so far. So just be careful and lock your doors."

Kayleigh snorted. "If he's going to come knocking on my door, he'll be one surprised burglar."

"Do not engage. This isn't a competition. If someone breaks into your house, you lock yourself in your room and call it in."

"Liam, I get that this is your job. But it will take at least fifteen minutes for a squad car to show up at my door. A lot of things can happen in that time. Don't worry about me. Worry about people like Phyllis or your mom. I can look after a dirtbag with sticky fingers."

"Kayleigh, can you not give me grief for one day?"

She came around the booth with a heaping spoon full of something. "Open up."

Against his better judgment, he did. She popped the spoon in his mouth and then slid it out, leaving the pie piece behind. He closed his eyes in bliss and chewed.

"Mrs. Baxter's Apple Brown Betty. Otherwise known as Mulberry's blue-ribbon winner. You're the first to know."

She put the ribbons on the first-, second-, and third-place winners, and also handed out a few honorable mentions. "That was worth all the extra calories."

"Where are you heading off to?" he asked. "Want to go on the Ferris wheel?"

"No, I'll puke." Kayleigh put her hand over her stomach. "I'm going to go home and get all prettied up for Winston Jones."

Liam fought not to grind his teeth. "Do you have a date?"

"No, but that's not going to stop me from trying to get one. Don't tell anyone, but I took one of the posters of him that was advertising the show and hung it up in my bedroom." She sighed. "I might have a small crush on Winston Jones."

Liam scowled. "He's got three ex-wives."

"Do you think he's looking for number four?" She batted her eyes at him.

"I think he's got his fair share of groupies."

"Yeah, I'm going to have to stand out in the crowd. What are you doing tonight?"

"Hopefully not arresting you for public indecency."

Crossing her arms over her chest, she glared at him. "What's that supposed to mean?"

"You're a respected member of the community. Don't make a fool out of yourself by acting like a silly teenager with a belly shirt and a skirt up to here." He gestured just below his hip. Images of her flirting with the country star filled his mind and Liam didn't like the emotions it was stirring up in him. This wasn't him.

"Are you trying to tell me how to dress now?"

The venom in her voice cut through the haze of jealousy he had been in. "No, of course not."

"Because it sounded like you were."

"I wasn't."

"But you think I'd look foolish in a short skirt and top?"

Liam wasn't sure he was going to be able to talk himself out of this one. "Can we forget I said that?"

"No."

Great.

"I'll dress however I want. And if you or any other members of the community have a problem with that, I can guarantee they will not like what I have to say to them." She stormed away.

"You know, Liam. You could have just asked her to go watch the draft horses with you. She's still horse crazy after all these years."

Liam turned to find Kayleigh's father looking at him, smiling. Obviously, he'd heard that whole exchange. Just when he thought it couldn't get any worse. He eyeballed the phone Jules carried. He hoped there weren't any more pictures of him and Kayleigh going up on Jules's social media. His mother was starting to get suspicious and the last thing he wanted was for Lila to approach Kayleigh. Liam didn't think his mother would be as blunt as his father had been when they'd been in high school, but he didn't want to put that idea to the test.

"Hey, Jules. I didn't mean any disrespect to Kayleigh."

"I know that."

"Things have been a little heated between us since the fireworks got cancelled. I suppose you're mad at me too?" Liam forced himself to meet Jules's eyes.

"Of course not. It's not a big deal to me. Would I like to go out on the boat with Leah and watch the fireworks like old times? Sure. But it's not going to ruin my summer if it doesn't happen."

"That's what I was trying to tell Kayleigh. The Fourth of July is just another day."

"Huh, no wonder you're at each other's throats." Jules covered a laugh with a cough. "It's not just another day for her. It's her favorite holiday. Telling her there'll be no fireworks for Independence Day is like not having gingerbread cookies at Christmas. But, most importantly, it reminds her of her mother. Giving up on this event, especially after last year's fiasco, is going to make her feel that she let her mother down."

The "again" was silent, but it was in between them.

"I didn't think of it that way," Liam said.

"You'll figure it out, son," he said. "Can I count on you to help fix up Kayleigh's kitchen?"

"Sure, whatever you need."

"Good man. I'll see you around. Don't let my daughter get you down."

Too late.

It was time for another birch beer, Liam decided. While he was filling up his mug, taking advantage of the unlimited free refills, Evan came up to him. "Got a minute?"

"Depends. Is this business or pleasure?"

"A little bit of both."

Liam followed Evan to the town council's tent. "I've been talking with the budget committee and they're willing to come together for a special meeting to allocate the firework funds into improving the fire department's trucks."

"What did Kayleigh say?" he asked.

"I haven't told her yet."

"Can I be there when you do?" That was going to be entertaining. Kayleigh would either hug Evan or hit him.

"I was hoping you could keep her occupied while we discuss it and vote. I want it to be a surprise."

"Oh, I can guarantee she'll be surprised, all right." Liam

rubbed his hand over his face.

"I know she wanted to have a fireworks display, but since we were handed this opportunity, I think we should use it to improve the safety of the town. Kayleigh can't argue that the trucks need upgrading."

"This seems a little sudden. What does the rest of the committee think?"

"They've got mixed emotions. But like I said before, no one wants another Chris Danvers situation. He got lucky. Maybe the next kid won't be."

"Preaching to the choir, Evan." Liam thought back on what Jules had just said. "She's going to want to argue her side."

"I don't want to muddy to vote."

"Seems sketchy," Liam said, frowning.

"It's not like I'm trying to embezzle funds. I'm doing this to help ease the disappointment of not having the fireworks show. If Kayleigh storms in, all guns ablazin', the chances that the budget committee will vote to spend the money on her department is slim. She's her own worst enemy some-times. You know that."

Liam sure did. Her temper didn't last long. It was like grenade. A big explosion and then nothing else. But it usually left destruction in its wake. "She's going to be disappointed about the fireworks."

"She'll get over it. Especially if it improves her depart-ment. Just keep her from buying fireworks and don't let her get suspicious. I want this to be a nice surprise for her. She's worked hard and has put a lot into this community. I want her to see this as a token of our gratitude and respect."

"You'd be better off spending the money on the fireworks, then," Liam said. "That's what she really wants."

"But the town would suffer. And that's not what any of us wants, including Kayleigh, after everything is said and done."

"I don't feel right about keeping this from her. The fireworks are tied up with her mother's death, and I'm afraid she's not going to see it any other way."

Evan took him by the arm and led him toward the booth that the army had set up.

"Kayleigh got shot up in Iraq. She didn't run and hide. She stood her ground and helped the wounded get out of a fire zone. She almost didn't make it."

Liam looked away. He'd heard the story from her sister Samantha, but he'd never had the nerve to ask Kayleigh about it. She must have been angry and frightened, but she did what she had to do, and she'd made it back home. Of course, the town was proud of her.

"What's your point?" Liam asked hoarsely.

"That aside from some lip service at local events, this town hasn't done a lot to show how much we appreciate her. Improving her department will last a lot longer than a forty-five-minute display. Can I count on you to keep this a secret until after the vote? I don't want her to sabotage this gift."

"I'll try." Liam wasn't sure how he was going to pull that off or if she would ever forgive him once she found out he knew about this and didn't tell her. But Evan was right. Kayleigh needed that money for fire department equipment more than the town needed fireworks.

LIAM DID NOT go home to get all prettied up for Winston Jones. In fact, he went back to the office and took two antacids. The peonies that he'd bought for Kayleigh were on Ada's desk. The fresh perfume of the flowers was sweet, and he was glad that someone was getting joy out of them.

He caught up on the reports and signed off on time sheets. He reviewed the latest robberies and racked his brain to come up with a pattern. Originally, Liam had put two squad cars in the parking lot of the summer festival, but now he was second-guessing himself. Wouldn't the thieves know that the townspeople would be distracted? This would be the perfect time to break into empty houses and cars.

"Hey, Chief," Cindy Herschel, one of his officers said, coming in from the end of her shift. "Did you hear that Old Lyme had a speeder with a bunch of illegal fireworks in the back of his truck? He had a bunch of sky flyers and display shells. But get this. They matched the lots of what was looted out of Tristar's warehouse."

"Sounds like a break in the case," Liam said.

"Nah, sounds like this guy bought them off a guy who bought them off a guy."

"Follow the money," Liam said. "It will eventually get to the end."

Remembering that Evan wanted more patrols for illegal fireworks displays here in Mulberry, Liam pulled one of the cars off festival duty and had him sit in the commuter lot to see if he noticed anything strange coming from or leaving the highway. Liam probably should do some patrolling as well. He made himself drink some Pepto-Bismol first to help his stomach recover from his day of eating like a twelve-year-old with a credit card. No regrets.

Liam winced as a pain jabbed into his abdomen. All right, maybe a few regrets.

While he waited for the medicine to coat his stomach, Liam clicked on the summer festival's website and searched out the promo shot of Winston Jones and his band. The link below it took him to a YouTube video of their greatest hits. They were pretty good. Liam bet they were going to put on an entertaining show. And maybe afterward, the boys in the band would have a party backstage and invite some pretty women to join them for a few drinks and dancing. If Winston Jones asked Kayleigh to leave with him, would that be the shove she needed to go?

Liam clicked off the video, but the summer festival website still showed Winston's head shot. They were going on in another hour. After glaring at the handsome cowboy's smiling face, Liam thumped his fist down on the desk.

"You're not getting my girl," he said.

"You say something, Chief?" Cindy asked from the back office.

"Nope." He hurried out before she called him out on the lie.

Chapter Twelve

KAYLEIGH WAS HAVING a good time up front at the Winston Jones concert. Leah and Samantha were dancing with her and singing along to the songs. She kept searching the crowd for Liam, which was stupid. He was probably on the Ferris wheel with Irene, who was probably dressed appropriately—whatever the hell that meant.

"You're scowling," Leah said, leaning in to shout in her ear.

"I'm just disappointed that Patty had to miss this," Kayleigh said, trying to push the annoying vision of Liam and Irene out of her mind.

"Trust me!" Samantha shouted. "The last place Patty wants to be right now is crammed into a hot, sticky crowd in front of the speakers. She's coming tomorrow to see the magic shows and acrobats."

Watching everyone have fun and jump around was a type of therapy to Kayleigh. Acting crazy and singing along to the band made her feel that normal was within reach. Coming back home in Mulberry seemed like the right decision, but she couldn't help feeling there was still something missing.

When the band took a break, Kayleigh and her sisters

made their way to the beer tent to get something cold and wet. Kayleigh's throat felt raw from screaming and hollering. While her sisters drank and caught up with their friends, she walked around to check out the other acts. Preacher Dan was up on the smaller stage. He had a guitar and a harmonica rig and was playing some Beatles tunes. Her dad and a bunch of his friends were hanging out, listening to him, and to her surprise, Kayleigh noticed that Irene was with them. She scanned the crowd for Liam, but didn't see him.

When she turned to go back to Winston Jones, figuring they were about to start their next set, she ran into Liam.

"Can I have this dance?" he said.

Looking around self-consciously, Kayleigh said, "Sure."

She stepped into his arms and they swayed to Preacher Dan's original song. At first, it was like being in junior high school again, stiff and enough space between them for a truck to run through. But as the song went on, they relaxed and got slightly closer. Her hand on his bicep and her other hand engulfed in his, felt right. She could get used to this.

Liam's hazel eyes held warmth and a smile for her. He smelled like spearmint, fresh and clean. Kayleigh wanted to hook her arm around his waist and lean her head on his shoulder, but she didn't want to break the fragile shell of intimacy that they had. She didn't see the crowd or hear anything but the song and the rapid beat of her heart.

They stared into each other's eyes. It had been like this once before when they were teenagers by the lake. They hadn't been dancing then. From what she remembered, they'd been on the floating raft trying to toss each other into the water. One moment it was all about the battle of wills, and the next, they both realized they were in bathing suits, wrestling skin to skin.

Kayleigh swallowed hard, remembering.

They had stayed there locked together for what had seemed like an eternity. Kayleigh had been too scared to break the intimacy. And then Liam leaned in and kissed her. Her first kiss. It had been sweet and innocent, and her heart had stopped beating in shock and delight. Then he shifted his weight and she knew he was going to use her distraction to toss her into the lake. So, she beat him to it.

Pulling away, she had slapped him across the face and then preemptively shoved him in the water. She hadn't noticed they'd had an audience until everyone started clapping. She swam back to shore and got yelled at by both their parents.

Reaching up, she stroked Liam's cheek. He startled, as if he was waiting for another slap.

"I shouldn't have hit you," she said.

Liam blinked at her and gave her a half smile. "Which time?"

Kayleigh felt like an idiot. Lost in her thoughts, she forgot that he couldn't actually read her mind. She entwined her arms around his neck. "Never mind. It was a long time ago."

She wondered if he even remembered that he'd kissed her. Kayleigh wondered how he would react if she kissed him first this time. She didn't want to ruin their comfortable friendship. That is, if bickering like an old married couple without the benefits counted as a relationship.

"You look pretty," he said, when she just smiled at the question in his eyes.

She wasn't sure if he was teasing her or not, so she responded as if he was. "So, I look appropriate?"

Liam rolled his eyes. "I'm trying to pay you a compliment."

"Why?" Kayleigh asked suspiciously. Was he setting her up for something?

"You know what? Never mind."

After a few beats of the song, she moved closer and rested her cheek on his chest. He stroked her hair as they swayed to the song.

"Aren't you two cute!" Jules said, taking a photo.

They sprang back to middle-school dance position. "Dad," she groaned.

Jules gave them a thumbs-up before going back to his group of friends.

"Sorry about that," Kayleigh said. "He's like a kid with a new toy with that phone."

"My mom's the same way," Liam said. "She stalks me around town, wondering why I'm not checking in. I told her because I'm a grown man, that's why."

"Not to mention, I'm sure all the bad guys would be interested in where the police chief was at any given moment. What are you doing here tonight? I figured you'd be working."

"I was. I am," he said defensively.

"Am I a suspect?"

"Probable cause," Liam said dryly. "Have you seen anything suspicious?"

"Aside from a few rigged games, not so much."

"Are you still cleaning up at darts?" Liam swung her around and she clung to his shoulders, laughing.

"If I had a need for a framed picture of a teddy bear, I'd be in like Flynn. Are you still knocking over milk jugs?"

"Why? Do you want a furry green monster that does not look like Oscar the Grouch because they can't afford the licensing fees?" He flexed his arm and she shamelessly ran her hand over his bicep.

"Everyone could use a stuffed animal they have to tie to the roof of their car to get it home," she said.

"Are you challenging me?" Liam said. "Because there might be a giant stuffed dog in your future."

"I'm sure Quinn would be terribly jealous."

"That dog." Liam sighed and shook his head. "How's the kitchen remodel coming?"

"The smell is finally gone. The contractors will be there tomorrow to give me an estimate, but it should be back to normal by the weekend. I got lucky."

"Next time, don't light candles."

"Is there going to be a next time?" she asked.

"I hope so. I was promised chicken cacciatore."

"It was the garlic bread that saved the kitchen."

"I've heard of the miracle properties of garlic."

"Well, maybe after the kitchen gets put back together, I can try again."

"I could come over and help cook dinner. Keep an eye

out for flying huskies and all that." Liam glanced down at her shyly.

She felt a flickering in her stomach that could be butterflies. "Sounds like a date," she said cautiously.

"It does, doesn't it?" His eyes dropped down to her lips, and for a wild moment, Kayleigh thought he was going to kiss her.

Just then, a distant boom sounded, and a red spidery firework appeared on the horizon. Kayleigh winced. "I suppose you're going to go after that."

"I've got cars on patrol," he said. "Unless it escalates, I'm staying here."

She glanced to the Bluetooth earpiece he wore and wondered if he was listening to his radio while they were dancing. "Where do you think they got their supply from?" she asked as a yellow one streaked into the air and exploded into a palm tree.

"Might have been from the looters. Old Lyme pulled over a pickup with a bed full of stolen Tristar fireworks. They're investigating now."

"Good." Kayleigh hoped the looters got punished. She couldn't get mad at Mother Nature for flooding Tristar's warehouse, but Mulberry would still be having their display if the thieves hadn't cleared them out.

As it was, she had less than five days to find replacement fireworks.

"You haven't found a supplier yet, have you?" Liam asked.

"Don't rub it in."

"Just let me know before you sign an agreement or give a verbal confirmation of the order."

"Why?"

"Can you let me do my job?" he said. "It's on me to follow procedures or ATF is going to be all in my business."

"Fine. You don't have to be such a control freak."

"Don't talk. Just dance."

Nodding, she relaxed into him and enjoyed the sway of his body to the sweet love song. Liam tugged her a bit closer, so their bodies brushed against each other. Kayleigh swallowed hard and looked everywhere but at him. It felt natural being in his arms, but there was a wildness to it as well. The brush of his raspy chin against her cheek made her heart stutter.

But of course, it couldn't last. The song was over, and they reluctantly broke apart and clapped. Irene and Kayleigh's father were suddenly next to them.

"Can I have this dance?" Irene said.

Liam shot Kayleigh a furtive look that she didn't know how to interpret and then said, "It would be my pleasure."

Kayleigh held in her sigh as Liam and Irene settled in to dance and fit together like it was perfectly natural. No awkwardness there.

"Dance with your old man," her father said.

"Can I stand on your feet like I used to?" She stepped on the tops of his large shoes.

"Are you still sixty pounds?" He grunted, shaking her off.

"It's not nice to ask a lady her age or her weight," Kayleigh said as she danced with her dad to a more upbeat song than the last one.

"It's a good thing I didn't raise any ladies." He twirled her around the fairgrounds.

This time, Kayleigh enjoyed seeing the lights on the ride, smelling the cotton candy and the buttered popcorn, and listening to the sounds of the crowd. It was exciting, and she felt like a little girl again.

"Is there something going on with you and Liam?"

"Just the usual," she said. "Are you upset that they cancelled the fireworks show?"

"If they don't have the fireworks, they can't have a show." He didn't seem to be concerned about it. Kayleigh wondered if Liam and Evan had been right—that no one really did care one way or another.

"Mom would have been so disappointed."

"Your mother wouldn't have given up."

"I'm not going to either," she said.

"Just cut Evan and Liam a break. They're just trying to do their jobs and keep everyone happy."

A blue chrysanthemum exploded into a trail of little sparks high in the sky. Out of the corner of her eye, she saw Liam excuse himself from his dance with Irene and tap his headset.

"I guess it escalated," she muttered.

"What's that all about?" her dad asked.

She told him about the stolen fireworks. "I'm hoping to be able to secure a vendor to supply us for Saturday night."

"Do Liam and Evan know about this?"

"Yeah, they're against it, but I'll get my way."

"One of these days, that's going to backfire on you," he warned.

"I just can't fathom not having the fireworks. It will be like I'm still waiting for summer to start."

"Well, when the pumpkins and the Christmas decorations come out, you'll come around to the idea."

"You know what I mean," she said.

"Go to another town's display. I bet that's what half of Mulberry is going to do. I hear New Haven puts on a nice show."

"It's not the same. Mom would never have let this happen."

"No," he agreed. "But she also wasn't the fire chief. You've got other things to worry about."

"Trust me, I'm worried about them. But I've got a great crew and we've got a handle on things."

"How are those trucks holding up?"

Kayleigh sagged. "It's a matter of time. The tanker needs a new engine and the ladder needs an upgrade."

"Let me know if I can do anything."

"I will. I'm keeping it running through sheer determination. I'm hoping that next year's budget will come through for a new truck."

"Because this town has a hundred and fifty thousand dollars lying around."

"They've got it," she scoffed. "Convincing them to spend it, on the other hand, is another story."

"Put your mind to it, like you're doing for these fireworks, and you'll get your new truck."

"I hope so," she said. The last thing she wanted was for

one of her trucks to break down during an emergency.

"Can you use the fireworks money to fix the truck?"

"Not without a vote from the budget committee, and I don't want to use that money for anything but what it was slated for."

"Seems silly to waste that much money on a show when it could keep your trucks rolling until the next budget is prepared."

She hated when her father had a point. "Well, that's not likely to happen. Evan avoids budget meetings like the plague. Could I come over and look through Mom's things? I know it's been almost a decade, but maybe some of her old contacts can help me out."

He shrugged. "You're welcome to come over anytime. Her things are in the attic. It's probably dusty as heck up there, and I wouldn't be surprised if there's a squirrel or two hiding nuts away for the winter."

"I want to keep the fireworks going as a tribute to Mom. That's why it's so important to me."

"I think she'd like that. But she wouldn't want you to lose sleep or break friendships over it."

"I won't," Kayleigh said, but she wondered if she was driving a wedge between herself and Liam.

"Nothing is going to take our memories of your mother away from us," her father said. "Whether we have a fireworks show at the end of the summer festival or if we have the high school band play show tunes, your mother will still be smiling down and watching over us."

"Thanks, Dad." She hugged him when the song ended and went back to find her sisters.

Chapter Thirteen

LIAM HAD THE day off and was happy to be in the food truck listening to Ada shout orders as if she were Gordon Ramsay. He had to step outside, though, when the onions and peppers got to be too much. Glancing over, he saw Kayleigh behind a long table, setting up an iced cooler with various chili condiments.

"Ada, are we ready for the lunch crowd?" Liam asked. It was eleven o'clock and the fairgrounds had only opened an hour ago, but he didn't want to miss another chance to defeat the firefighters. Their chili game was fierce, but he thought they could win this year because Ada's mother had finally given up her secret chili recipe. He hoped it wasn't too hot for the Mulberry crowd.

"We're ready. We were born ready," she called out and her family and the other off-duty officers who were helping out hooted and shouted.

Liam walked over to Kayleigh. They had two types of chili this year—a white chili with chicken and white beans, and a steak-and-three-bean chili that Liam was dying to try. He tossed a five-dollar bill into the jar and accepted a bowl topped with a few tablespoons of shredded cheese and a dollop of sour cream.

"Admitting defeat this early in the game?" Kayleigh asked.

"Just checking out the competition." Taking a tentative taste, his taste buds jumped for joy. He decimated the rest while Kayleigh looked on, smirking. "Adequate." He tossed the empty plastic bowl in the trash.

Hurrying back to the police food truck, he said, "We're in trouble." He made sure to keep his voice down. "Their steak chili is the best I've ever tasted."

Ada snorted. "We'll see about that." She gave him a bowl and put a serving spoonful of fragrant beans and meat in it. "It's not steak, but I don't think you'll notice."

Liam scooped some up. It was tasty, and he really appreciated the slow burn that built up after a few bites. He grabbed some corn chips to keep the heat under control. "That's really good too."

The firefighters' chili was better, but he'd never say that to Ada. It was a good thing that all the money they were raising would go to the food bank and other charitable causes, so Liam didn't have to feel guilty about spending another five dollars on the white chicken chili this time.

"Back again?" Kayleigh said.

"I told you, I've got to test out the competition," he said defensively. This time, he took a few sprigs of cilantro with his glop of sour cream. There wasn't any heat in this chili. The green peppers were mild. But the sauce was savory and creamy. The chicken was tender and juicy and the cannellini beans made it a hearty meal.

They were doomed. Completely doomed. But Liam

wasn't about to give up without a fight. He knew he'd have to market their chili to the bold and the heat lovers. That's where Ada's chili would reign.

As lunchtime got closer, the lines were getting longer. Liam and his team dished out chili and collected the money, while Ada managed the cooking side of things. They had several Crock-Pots and stockpots going, but it was hard to keep up with demand. In the end, they sold out before three p.m., but the firefighter team was still going.

"Did we just sell out faster?" Ada said.

"It's like they've got a never-ending supply of chili," Cindy said, wiping her hands on a towel.

Sure enough, he saw Leah and her father rushing to the back of the truck carrying Crock-Pots.

"I think that's cheating," Zach said. "And the health department is going to get them if they're not making those in a commercial kitchen."

Liam pointed his chin toward another car that had pulled up behind the food truck. Ginny Stevens, the owner of the Lobster Dock restaurant, got out and produced a stockpot out of the back of her SUV. "Looks like they got one."

"Why didn't we think of that?" Ada said, crossing her arms.

"We didn't think the chili would be that popular," Liam said. "Not with all the other concession stands around."

He had to hand it to Kayleigh. She had outmaneuvered him. When she'd mentioned she'd rented food trucks for them to work out of, so they wouldn't have to rely on a commercial kitchen, he assumed that they weren't going to use one in addition to the trucks. He'd remember that for next time. Tipping his water bottle in her direction, he saluted her victory. She gave him a little curtsey to acknowledge it.

"Maybe next time we should do an ice cream booth," Cindy said.

When the chili line finally ran dry, the firefighters had outsold the police officers three-to-one. But they'd all managed to bring in seven thousand dollars for charity.

"That's a lot of chili bowls," Liam said. "I guess we should have known not to go up against a firehouse with chili recipes."

Kayleigh came up and patted him on the back. "It was a good effort. Ada's recipe was amazing. It was a little too hot for me, but I could appreciate the flavor."

"Yours were great too. Good job on the extra help with Ginny. It could have backfired on you, though, and then you'd have been stuck with a lot of extras."

"Nah, we'd freeze some and then donate the rest to the soup kitchens. It would be chili night for everyone."

No wonder he sometimes got tongue-tied around her. She thought of everything.

"I'm going to walk around the festival to burn some chili calories off. Want to join me?" he asked.

"Sure." She hooked her arm in his and they headed in the direction of the midway. "Are you hungry?"

Liam groaned. "I don't think I'm ever eating again. Until dinner, that is. Or if I smell the fried-dough pizzas."

"It's a good thing the summer festival is only one week a year," she said. "Otherwise I'd have to be doing a lot more sprints in my gear."

"There's an idea for another competition. Relay races in our gear."

Kayleigh scoffed. "Like that's fair. My gear is over fifty pounds."

"This gun belt weighs about twenty. Add a tactical vest and body armor and I bet we could get a comparable weight."

"We'd have to have an official gear weigh-in."

"Naturally," he said.

"I think we've found a new event for next summer's festival."

Liam liked that she was talking about the future and next summer. He wondered if she was coming to terms with the fireworks show not being the finale of the event. He knew it would always have meaning for her, but he wanted her to have something of her own for the summer festival. Or maybe he was just being selfish, and wanted her to have something to share with him that would build memories and a connection to him.

"Are you still thinking of leaving Mulberry?" he asked, dreading the answer.

"Not as often as I have been," Kayleigh admitted. "I think it might be time to stop running."

Liam's heart thudded in relief. It was time for him to stop running too. He was going to ask her out and tell his mother to butt the heck out. Liam took her father's advice and steered her over to the livestock area. He wasn't sure of the schedule, but he thought the draft horse competition was sometime soon.

"So, any luck on the firework thieves?" she asked.

"Not that I've heard," he said. "We had another rash of cars broken into last night. All of them were unlocked. It happened around two in the morning, and we've got grainy camera pictures. It looks like they're coming in one car, then going out on foot to scour the neighborhoods. If the car is locked, they move on. If it's not, they search it and take whatever they can sell."

"Going for low-hanging fruit."

"Yeah, but what happens when everyone starts locking their cars? I want to nip this in the bud now, before it escalates."

"You'll do it," she said. "Maybe we should rally up a neighborhood watch."

"I don't want to scare people and I don't want people to put themselves in harm's way. Right now, there haven't been any weapons used, and no one has gotten hurt. Let the police handle it."

"All right," Kayleigh said. "Stop being so defensive."

"I'm not defensive." He helped her up onto the temporary risers that acted like bleachers over the horse rink.

"That's a Clydesdale and that's a Percheron," Kayleigh said, pointing to two enormous horses. "I like the Percherons best."

"Isn't that sacrilege for a firefighter? Didn't the Clydesdales pull the steam-powered pumpers?"

"No, they pulled beer wagons." Kayleigh laughed. "Percherons were usually used by fire departments. They were trained so well that when they heard the fire alarm, they would come out of their stalls and line up in the exact position to get their harnesses on."

"I remember when you wanted an Appaloosa."

"I loved the spots."

"You guys should get a dalmatian for the fire house, if you like spots so much."

She shook her head. "I don't need another thing to worry about. Besides, I'd miss him when I wasn't sleeping at the firehouse."

Liam's cell phone rang, and he glanced down at it. Evan. "Be right back," he said, and hopped down from the bleachers to take the call.

"Yeah?" he said, walking out of Kayleigh's hearing.

"Good news. The board voted to use the current twenty-five thousand to upgrade the fire trucks."

Liam wasn't sure that was going to be good news to Kayleigh. She was counting on that money for the fireworks. "What about the deposit?"

"We're going to cross that bridge once we have the money back in hand."

Which could take several months. But that meant Kayleigh no longer had a fireworks budget. If she found a vendor, she'd be paying it out of pocket. He had to tell her.

"Thanks for letting me know."

"I'm going to call Kayleigh next."

"No," Liam shouted, and it was loud enough that

Kayleigh looked his way and frowned. She got up and was heading toward him. "I'm with her right now."

"Great. Let me talk to her."

"Uh," Liam said. "I think I should tell her in person."

"No, this is my idea and I want her to hear it from me."

"What's going on?" Kayleigh said. "Is something wrong?"

Feeling like a coward, Liam sighed. "Evan wants to talk to you." He handed her his phone.

"Evan?" she asked warily.

Liam watched the range of emotions cross her face while she listened to Evan tell her about going behind her back to get the budget committee to give the fireworks money to the fire department. It was just like when he'd first told her that the show had been cancelled. Only this time, he saw disbelief, rage, sadness, and finally, acceptance.

"I see," she said.

Not knowing what to do, Liam just stood there. He wanted to put a hand on her shoulder to comfort her, but if she shrugged it off, he'd be devastated.

"That's very generous of the committee." Her voice was a flat monotone. "Thank you very much for thinking of me. The money will definitely come in handy. I'll have some quotes for you on your desk by Monday."

Expressionless, Kayleigh handed him back the phone.

"Kayleigh," he said.

"Did you know he was doing this?"

"Yeah."

"Why didn't you tell me? I could have at least tried to sway the budget committee's mind."

"I thought this was a better use of the money."

She clamped her mouth shut and squeezed her eyes closed.

"Are you counting to ten?" he asked.

"Ten's not enough," she gritted out.

"Go on and yell at me, then. I can take it." He'd rather have her yell at him than the icy politeness she was showing.

She took a deep breath and opened her eyes. "I'm not going to throw a tantrum like a toddler in the middle of the fairgrounds."

"We can go in my car, if you like," he said.

"I just need to go. I need some time alone to process this."

"Process what?"

"Everything."

Kayleigh started walking away, but Liam couldn't let her storm off feeling like this. Did she think he'd betrayed her? Had he? "Kayleigh, this is a good thing for the town."

"I know," she said raggedly. "Just leave me alone."

"Liam," Irene Mulberry called from over by the chickens. "I need you. Can you come here for a moment?"

"Perfect," Kayleigh said between her teeth and sped up.

Caught between chasing after her and ignoring Irene, Liam stopped in his tracks.

"I think my purse has been stolen," Irene said.

That helped with his decision. Duty called.

Chapter Fourteen

T HE NEXT DAY, Kayleigh broke the good news about the money to her team, keeping her mixed feelings to herself. She tried to keep her father's words in mind, but it still felt like a betrayal to her mother's memory, and her restlessness was suddenly back, making her doubt her decision to stay in Mulberry. She assigned Hank and her lieutenant to research companies and parts that they would need.

"Call my dad or Samantha, if you need specifics. They know these trucks just as well or even better than I do."

"What are you up to today?" Hank asked.

It was her day off. "I'm going to head down to the dunking booth," she said. It was Liam and Evan's turn today. She planned on throwing softballs at the target until her arm gave out. Hopefully, by that time, she wouldn't be as angry at them as she was.

But before she went to the fairgrounds, she stopped at her dad's house. He was at the shop with Samantha, but Kayleigh had an extra key. After letting herself in, she went up to the attic. Climbing the stairs, she reached up to pull the cord that lit up the bare light bulb. The attic was dusty all right, but she didn't see any evidence of rodent activity.

Kayleigh located the steamer chest with her mother's things and opened it. It was basically a memory box of her life. It smelled like lavender and cedar, scents Kayleigh associated with her mother. She wasn't sure why she was here. After all, even if there was a ten-year-old contact that could help her, Kayleigh no longer had the budget to buy any fireworks.

"Sorry, Mom," she said, her finger tracing her parents' framed wedding picture. Pulling out her mother's scrapbook, Kayleigh put it on her lap. It was filled with cutouts of the packaging of Johanna's favorite fireworks and firework companies. The scrapbook documented Johanna's journey to becoming a licensed shooter. It showed her apprenticeship, where she dug holes and checked and rechecked the circuits for rigging up electronic shows. Her mother had to study chemistry as well as electricity and had become an expert in the field.

Kayleigh had wanted to apprentice with her and had planned to do it after she got back from her tour of duty. But by that time, everything had changed. Kayleigh had seen her share of battles in the Middle East. Her mother had passed away. Patty had just gotten married. Her sisters had their own careers. And Liam had become distant. After leaving the army, she didn't feel like she could live in Mulberry anymore.

But after ten years of not fitting in anywhere else, Kayleigh finally came back home, needing some familiarity and comfort in traditions. It was good the first year, and she felt that she was making some progress into finding the new normal.

But now, she was off-kilter again.

The only thing she could think of was to raise some money and drag Liam by the ear to Pennsylvania to buy some shells from those roadside stands. He had a permit, so it wouldn't be illegal to possess them or to take them across state lines if they were for a show. Kayleigh wasn't a licensed shooter, but she could rig up a display. It wouldn't be the best show, but it would be something. Unfortunately, she didn't have a couple thousand dollars lying around.

Too bad the confiscated fireworks Old Lyme found were evidence in a criminal case. She could have seen if Liam would negotiate that they be destroyed on the Fourth of July here on the Mulberry green.

With a last sigh, Kayleigh put everything back the way she'd found it and decided to go home instead of to the summer festival. She didn't want to be around happy people at the moment.

Unfortunately, when she got home, the contractors were working in her kitchen. Leah was eating a sandwich standing up. That's what happened when you didn't have a table anymore.

"What are you doing here?" Kayleigh asked. Her family had keys to her house, just as she had keys to theirs.

"You weren't answering your phone, so Dad sent me here to let these guys in."

"My battery is dead," she said, pulling it out of her pocket. With all the hammering going on, it didn't seem like she was going to get any peace and quiet.

"Have you picked out a new table or chairs yet?"

Kayleigh shrugged. "I figured I go with the same set I got at Ikea. It's still in stock."

"Do you want to go pick it up now? We can take my truck."

"Sure," Kayleigh said. "Just let me grab my phone charger."

On the way, she told Leah about the budget committee's decision.

"Wow, how are you supposed to feel about that?" Leah said. "On one hand, they completely erased Mom's legacy in this town. On the other, they supported the fire department with a much-needed boost."

"I know."

"There's got to be a way to do both."

"Not without spending a boatload of cash."

They walked into the big warehouse store. Kayleigh could get lost in here. If only her life could be put together in nice organized baskets in streamlined wood furniture. She liked the minimalist lifestyle in theory—it was nice to look at—but in her heart, she was the queen of clutter.

"Come on," Leah said, dragging her past a shelving unit that would require a lot of swearing to put together.

They located the table and, together, lifted it and put it on the large rolling cart, along with four chairs that also needed to be put together. Thinking about it, Kayleigh grabbed a fifth one.

"Who's that for?" Leah asked.

Kayleigh shrugged, not wanting to look too closely at her

decision. "For pizza night."

"You only need four chairs for the family. If you want enough chairs for your crew, you're going to need a bigger table."

"I just want another chair. Don't make a big deal about it," Kayleigh said, almost ready to put it back.

Leah grunted, but let the subject drop. Together they pushed the cart toward the registers.

"Do you girls need any help?" one of the workers said.

Kayleigh was going to let the "girls" remark go, but Leah wasn't wired that way.

"Girls?" Leah said. "Really? Next, you're going to ask us if we want to pay for someone to put this together for us."

"Do you?" the worker brightened, apparently thinking he could get a nice commission off this purchase.

Kayleigh closed her eyes and sat down on the nearest chair. This was going to take a while. She watched while her youngest sister gave an abbreviated version of life growing up with their father to the poor, young man who obviously hadn't paid attention in his corporate sensitivity training.

"So, not only was I changing tires when I was sixteen, I was building garage storage racks in my spare time." Leah was winding down.

Kayleigh jumped up and said, "Thanks anyway, but we've got this."

After they paid and loaded up the truck, they headed back to her house. The contractors were still there, and Kayleigh wasn't too proud to ask them to help them unload.

"We could have managed on our own," Leah said, as

they all stacked the flat boxes into the living room.

"Yeah, but we didn't have to." Kayleigh was all about making use of the resources you had. Of course, staring at all the stuff she had to put together, she suddenly didn't want to do it.

Leah pushed by her and opened the box that had the table pieces. "Get your tools."

Then again, sometimes you didn't get a choice. As she headed out into the garage, her phone rang. It was Liam. She ignored it. She wasn't ready to talk with him yet. Grabbing her toolbox, she came back into the living room where Leah was staring at the instructions in disgust.

"Why do they even bother with these?" Leah waved them at her.

Her phone buzzed again. Kayleigh shut it off.

"Who was that?"

"Liam, or maybe it was Evan. I didn't check."

"Are you mad at them?"

"I'm trying not to be. I know they had my best interests and the community at heart. It just makes me angry that I wasn't allowed to plead my case to the budget committee."

"I'd let Liam off the hook, but I'm still mad at Evan after what he pulled with Samantha."

Kayleigh frowned. No one messed with her sisters. "What did he do?"

"Do you remember Evan's ex, Corrine Brooks?"

"Vaguely. Isn't she an Instagram influencer or something?"

"That's her. Well, she's getting married and invited Evan

to the wedding. Only Evan stupidly told her that he was engaged, and now he has to come up with a fake fiancée. Guess who he asked?"

"Please don't tell me it was Samantha, because she's 'safe' and won't get the wrong idea that Evan is anything but a confirmed bachelor."

"Got it in one."

"He's a jerk. He knew better than to ask me to be his fake fiancée. Although, I might have said yes just to mess with him," Kayleigh said.

"Anyway, Samantha's in a tizzy because she thinks she might be able to bring in some new business for the auto repair shop, so now, she's trying to outshine the Instagram queen."

"I changed my mind," Kayleigh said. "Let's go to the summer festival. Evan's in the dunking booth today. We can put the table together later."

Leah shoved everything back in the box.

When they got to the festival, they bought twenty dollars' worth of tickets each, and then went right for the dunking booth where they traded the tickets in for a few buckets of balls.

Liam was sitting on the platform in swimming trunks. Kayleigh tried not to admire his toned legs and six-pack abs. "I was waiting for you to show up," he said. And the idiot looked relieved.

Her first throw missed.

"You might want to warm up your arm first before you go throwing all out like that," he said. "You'll blow out your shoulder."

"Thanks for the advice," she said and rolled her arm around for a few seconds. She let Leah go ahead of her and her sister streamed in two fast ones that were nowhere near the bullseye. In fact, they hit right about where his head would have been if it hadn't been for the steel link fence protecting him from stray balls.

"Bloodthirsty," Liam said.

"Come out here and say that," Leah said. "Or better yet, come out on the boat with me. I need some bait for my lobster pots."

"Are you threatening a police officer?" Liam grinned.

"Of course not. I'm inviting you out for a nice day out on the water."

"Uh-huh. No thanks. I hear there are great white sharks out by the edges of the harbor."

"You got nothing to worry about, unless you're a seal. Or unless you decide to take a dip in the ocean."

"Okay, my turn." Kayleigh pushed Leah out of the way.

This time, she hit the bullseye and plunged Liam into the icy pool. He kicked up right away and pulled himself back on the platform. Again, she tried not to notice the flex of his arm muscles or how his bathing suit clung nicely in all the right places.

"When are you getting in here?" Liam asked, pushing the hair out of his eyes.

"Nobody would pay to knock me in the drink."

"I would," Liam said. "And it's for a good cause."

Kayleigh looked at the bulletin board next to the cage.

The money was going toward school supplies for under-served towns in Connecticut. It was a good cause. How many kids could be helped with twenty-five thousand dollars?

She missed the next throw.

"Strike one."

And the next. Maybe it was selfish to have a grand fireworks program when people were suffering. Maybe the money was better off spent in the community.

"Strike two."

She wished she could talk to her mother about this.

"That the best you got?" Liam taunted.

As Kayleigh dunked him with the third shot, a new idea started to form. Just because they didn't have any "official" money from the town, that didn't mean they couldn't have a fireworks show. Sure, it would be an even smaller show than she had been planning, but she had helped her mother design shows all through her teens. She would just need a licensed shooter to set them off safely. And she had a few army buddies she might be able to call who had their permits and were licensed.

"That water is frigid," he said, coming up. "I thought it would feel good, but it's like ice."

She dunked him again, before he could even get settled on the platform. It felt good. She wondered if Liam would be on board now that the money was being spent for the community instead of a large show. She knew her buddies would donate their time to setting the fireworks off safely. Her family would donate some money. They could have it all. Kayleigh smiled.

"Not nice," Liam said. "I swallowed some water that time."

Liam made it back to the platform, but only because she missed her next throw. "If you kept your mouth shut, that wouldn't happen," she said.

"How long are you going to keep this up?" he asked.

"Keep what up?" She grunted. Missed again.

"You know what."

Bullseye, back into the pool.

"I'll let you know." Kayleigh held off on her next pitch because Evan was approaching. He had on a bathing suit and flip-flops, with a towel around his shoulders. Pulling on a pair of swim goggles, he asked, "Do you think I'll need these?"

"Yes," Kayleigh and Leah said.

Chapter Fifteen

LIAM TOWELED OFF, but didn't stay around to see the carnage the Baker sisters were going to inflict on Evan. He went into the dressing room and changed back into his regular clothes. He had a chill and for July, that was unusual. He hoped he wasn't coming down with something. He felt "off," but that could be because he didn't know where he stood with Kayleigh. She had every reason to be mad at him, but he didn't want her to be. And he didn't know how to fix it.

As he was walking back to his car, there was a commotion over by the ambulances. He saw Patty Martin being slid into the back and he sprinted over.

"Patty, are you all right?"

"She's going into labor," one of the paramedics said.

"Is your family with you?" Liam asked Patty. "Can I call someone?"

"They're on the rides somewhere," Patty said, breathing heavily. "My mom. My sister and her husband and their kids."

"We've got to go now, Chief."

Liam hopped into the ambulance and called Kayleigh, praying that she would pick up the phone this time instead of dodging him, like she'd been doing all day.

"Is this important? Because I'm on low battery," she said when she answered.

"Patty's in labor. I'm in the ambulance with her heading toward Yale. Her family is on the rides. Can you round them up and meet us at the hospital?" He talked fast, hoping she'd understand the urgency.

"Yes," she said and hung up.

It wasn't the warm and fuzzy conversation he had been hoping for, but at least she was talking with him again.

Liam held Patty's hand. "Kayleigh's going to find them and bring them to the hospital."

Patty started to cry. "I want Tully."

"Is he in port?" Liam asked.

"N-no."

"Who's Tully?" the paramedic asked.

"He's her husband. He's deployed on a sub." Liam turned back to Patty. "Don't worry, we'll get a message to him that his son or daughter is on the way."

"Daughter," she said, still sniffling.

"It's going to be all right," Liam said. "But you need to concentrate on your little one right now. Kayleigh and I will take care of everything."

"I'm glad the two of you are finally together."

Liam's breath caught in his throat. He wished. "What do you mean?"

Patty gripped his hand hard as a contraction hit her.

He immediately felt like a callous jerk for interrogating her, considering she was literally giving birth.

JAMIE K. SCHMIDT

But Patty seemed to want the distraction because after the contraction passed, she sagged against the stretcher and said, "You are so comfortable with each other—when you stop bickering, that is. You're good for her. You remind her that she has a past here, that she belongs here." Patty held her breath.

"Breathe," the paramedic said.

Patty exhaled, adding an ear-splitting scream.

"How much longer?" Liam glanced up front to see how close to the hospital they were.

"You ever delivered a baby, Chief?"

Liam swallowed hard and swayed. He'd taken the training, but had never actually done it before.

"Stay with me." The paramedic put a steadying hand on him. "I need you to keep her calm. Don't worry, Patty. I'm trained to deliver babies."

"G-good," she said. "I'm scared."

That snapped Liam back into reality. "Don't be scared, Patty. Everything is going to be all right."

"Kayleigh's my birth coach. I wish she was here."

Liam called Kayleigh.

"I've got Patty's mom and sister in Leah's truck with me. We're on our way," Kayleigh said.

"Is your phone plugged in?"

"Yeah, why?"

"Your best friend needs her birth coach." Still holding on to Patty's hand, Liam held the phone up to Patty's ear. Liam couldn't hear what Kayleigh was saying to her, but Patty started to laugh and cry at the same time. And then she screamed again as another contraction hit her.

"You're doing great," the paramedic said. "Start your breathing exercises now."

Liam could hear the steady drone of Kayleigh's voice, and he and Patty breathed together in time.

"I can see the baby's head," the paramedic said.

"But we're not at the hospital yet." Liam forced his voice to sound calm.

"They're waiting for us. But we're not waiting for them, are we, Patty? You can push now."

Patty bore down and pushed.

Liam was losing feeling in his hand. "You can do this, Patty. You're doing great."

It seemed like forever, but with a few more pushes and a lot of screaming, Patty's baby girl squalled her greeting to the world. The paramedic cut the cord and cleaned up the baby. By the time the ambulance arrived at the hospital, mom and baby were cuddled up close to each other. As they were wheeled into the hospital, Liam wasn't sure if his legs were going to support him, so he hung out in the back of the ambulance.

About ten minutes later, Kayleigh poked her head in. "Are you going to make it?"

"I don't know," he said honestly, but reached out for her hand and let her pull him out of the ambulance. She gave him a big hug, and he wasn't sure, but she was probably supporting him from falling on his face.

"The baby is beautiful," Liam said. "Perfect. Patty was so brave."

"Thank you," Kayleigh said, choking on tears. "Thank you so much for being there for her."

KAYLEIGH WRESTLED LIAM into a chair in the waiting room, and helped Patty's mother and sister get Patty and the baby settled into a room. Patty named the baby Ayesha after Tully's mother. Now this was a remembrance, not an annual fireworks show. Kayleigh was starting to feel a little ridiculous at all the fuss she'd been making. So what if tradition was broken? New traditions started all the time. She looked down at the sleeping baby. Liam had been right. Ayesha was perfect.

The doctors checked both Ayesha and Patty out and reported that both were doing great. Kayleigh stepped out to give them some privacy and called Leah, whom she had stranded at the summer festival.

"No worries. Hank is giving me a ride home. We're swinging by your place to check on the contractors and lock up."

"Okay. I'll be back soon. I'll take Liam home because he was in the ambulance with Patty. It should have been me. I was her birth coach."

"It all worked out in the end. Don't beat yourself up about it."

"Yeah." Kayleigh ran her fingers through her hair. "I'll talk with you later." Maybe if she hadn't been so hurt about the fireworks, she would have been with Patty and her family today, instead of taking potshots at Evan. Feeling guilty, she went and got Liam a cup of coffee. He liked it black, no cream or sugar. She couldn't imagine anyone enjoying something that bitter, and got herself a café mocha, because everything was better when you added chocolate to it.

"Thanks," he said, and when their fingers brushed, they tingled.

Sitting next to him, her leg rested against his as he was sprawled out in the chair. "You look beat. Do you want me to see if Ada or someone can pick you up?"

"I'll ride back with you, if you don't mind." He looked over the rim of his coffee cup at her, as if he expected her to argue.

"Of course you can. I'm going to be here for a while, though."

"I'm good where I am for now. I don't mind waiting. Especially since you brought me coffee. I could stand to recharge my batteries a bit. I've been on the go nonstop for the last couple weeks. If it wasn't setting up for the summer festival, it was investigating these burglaries."

"Yeah, I know. Good. Stay here and rest." Kayleigh stood up. "I'm going back up to check on Patty. When you're ready, though, come up and see her and the baby."

"I don't want to intrude," he said.

"You were there when Ayesha was born. You're not intruding."

"Okay."

Kayleigh spent a few more hours making sure that Patty and the baby had everything they needed. Patty's brother-in-law was dropping the kids off with a sitter, and then was coming to the hospital. Liam finally got his legs back under him and showed up. He received hugs from everyone and got to hold the baby for a little while until it was time for Patty to nurse. Then, he turned red as a beet and looked up at the ceiling as if it was the most fascinating thing ever.

"Let's get you home," Kayleigh said. "Patty, you did good. I'll see you later. Call me if you need anything."

"Thank you both so much," Patty said. "Ayesha, say goodbye to Auntie Kayleigh and Uncle Liam."

Kayleigh smiled at the baby and then slung an arm around Liam. "Let's go and give them some privacy and time to rest."

"Yeah," Liam said.

"You look a little shell-shocked. Are you going to be okay?"

"Yeah."

"Uh-huh." Kayleigh kept her arm around him until they got into the truck. "You're supposed to be a big, bad cop with all this training and one little birth takes the wind out of you."

"It's a lot different up close than it is watching on a training video and working on a mannequin. The mannequins don't yell that loud. I think I'm partially deaf."

"You'll recover. You did great, by the way."

"Thanks. Quick work on your part too. How did you round up her family so fast?"

"I had help. I grabbed a microphone and made announcements and everyone with a megaphone went around the festival looking for them."

Liam was too quiet on the drive back to his car at the fairgrounds. By now, the festival was getting into evening mode. More bands would be playing tonight, but Kayleigh just wanted a quiet evening at home. Hopefully, the contractors had finished, and her sisters weren't at her house putting together her kitchen table and chairs.

"Do you need me to drive?" She parked alongside his squad car. "I will as long as I can flip on the lights and sirens."

He smiled. "No, I'm good. I just wanted to apologize for not telling you about the budget vote. Evan asked me not to, but I should have refused. I didn't want the money used for fireworks, but you should have been given an opportunity to argue your point of view."

"It probably wouldn't have gone my way anyway," Kayleigh said.

"So, do you forgive me?"

"Yeah, we're good." She took a deep breath. "If I can get some money together, will you go to Pennsylvania with me to buy some fireworks, since you're the permit holder for the town?"

"No." He shook his head. "It's too dangerous to carry those loads in a car."

"I'm not going to get that much money together on such short notice," she said. "What I'll be able to buy will be fine in a trunk."

"Just let it go for this year," Liam said. "We've already had so much on our plate . . . Let's have the end of the summer festival be one without noise complaints or pets running away."

"If we do that, we risk another Chris Danvers incident." At this point, Kayleigh knew they were still circling around the old arguments, but she hoped that he'd realize it wasn't that big a deal. Unfortunately, she was getting the feeling that he thought the same about her.

"Kids are going to play with fireworks whether we have the show or not," he said. Liam sounded exhausted and she couldn't blame him.

She was sick of this too. But she couldn't resist just one more try. "There's going to be noise complaints and pets running away whether we have the show or not as well."

"I don't want to fight about this."

"I don't either." Okay. It was plan B, then. She had to see which one of her army buddies was free.

After a moment, Liam slid out of the truck. "I'll see you tomorrow."

"Take it easy." She watched him drive away. She was disappointed that he couldn't support her with even this small thing. But she didn't have the energy to be mad at him anymore. She had to let it go if she wanted to move their relationship beyond friendship. Patty was right about one thing—someone had to give in. This was her way of giving in. She'd just have to find a work-around.

Chapter Sixteen

THE NEXT DAY, Kayleigh worked a twelve-hour shift at the firehouse. She washed the trucks with the crew, checked the equipment, and set the schedule for the next two weeks. After work, she grabbed a six-pack and headed over to where Leah's boat was docked in the town marina.

Her sister was cleaning up after taking a few fishermen out to Half Acre and back. Kayleigh grabbed a mop and started swabbing the deck, like her mother had taught all of them.

"I want to see my face shining in that brass," Leah said.

"Then you better do it yourself," Kayleigh retorted, something she never would have said to her mother. But after she was done mopping, she did grab a cleaning rag and helped wipe everything down.

"What brings you out here as unpaid help?" Leah asked.

"I wanted to thank you for the use of your truck."

"No problem. I'm just glad Patty and the baby are doing all right."

"They're going to send her home tomorrow."

"Man, that's quick." Leah shook her head in disbelief.

"I'd rather be home than in a germy hospital."

"I guess."

"So, let me ask you a question."

"I knew there had to be a catch." Leah hoisted herself up into the captain's chair.

"I'm thinking of driving to Pennsylvania and buying a couple thousand dollars' worth of fireworks and then bringing them back here to be set off on Fourth of July."

"That's illegal."

"Not the way I'm planning it," Kayleigh said.

Leah put her legs up on the first mate's seat. "This ought to be good. Let's hear the plan."

"I've got a buddy from the army who has a permit to buy fireworks and transport them across state lines as long as the destination is a state that allows them."

"Connecticut does not allow aerial fireworks. Unless you were planning on getting the wussy ground ones."

"I wouldn't have to go all the way to Pennsylvania for those," Kayleigh scoffed. "If Evan agrees to put the fireworks show back on the summer agenda, then we can bring the big shells into town specifically for that show. Beck is also a licensed shooter, so we can set them off electronically, as we normally would with Tristar. The town gets their show without having to pay for it and everybody's happy."

"Let's back this up a bit. What if Evan won't put it back on the agenda?"

"Then it's illegal."

"And are you still going to go through with it?"

"I haven't thought that far yet. I'm wondering if it's better to ask for forgiveness than permission."

"Not in this case," Leah said. "And you know that."

Kayleigh groaned. "Yeah, I do."

"Why don't you ask Liam to go with you? That way it won't be illegal at all. He's the one who has to sign off on the fireworks once they get to town, no matter what Evan says."

"Actually, Beck would be the permit holder so it would be his responsibility, not Liam's."

Leah glared at her. "You're trying to keep the chief of police out of this?"

"He doesn't want any part of it. It could be a fire department thing."

"And you told all of this to Liam?"

"I asked him to come with me to pick up the fireworks. He said no, because he doesn't want there to be a show."

"And you accepted that?" Leah scoffed. "Here's the deal. I'll give you some money for fireworks out of my business account." She held up a hand to stop Kayleigh's cheer. "But only if I can use it as a tax write-off. And in order for me to do that, the town has to approve the show, and the fireworks have to be bought legally. That means Liam can't be cut out of the loop. He has a job to do and he can't do it if you circumvent him. Mom wouldn't want you to do that."

Kayleigh sighed. "Yeah, I know. I was trying to convince myself that the ends justify the means."

"They don't. And you know better."

"You're right."

"Don't look so defeated. I know you can get Evan and Liam to change their minds."

"I haven't been able to so far."

"Try harder," Leah said.

"Easy for you to say." She drank a few beers with her sister and helped her finish cleaning up the boat. Then Kayleigh went over to the Baker & Daughters Auto Repair shop. Technically, Samantha was the only daughter on the payroll, but Kayleigh and Leah could tune up a car in a pinch, so her father left the sign as is.

Samantha had her head under the hood of a car, but her father was in his office. She decided that Leah had a point—it wasn't worth going behind Liam's back. "Dad, if I can convince Evan to have the fireworks show go on and if Liam agrees, would you donate some money to buy the fireworks? It'll be tax deductible."

"Are you still on this?" her father asked.

"You know me. I can't let anything go."

"Fine, but I'm not cutting you a check until you get Liam and Evan on board."

"Did someone mention Evan?" Samantha came in, wiping her hand on a rag.

Kayleigh glanced at her father, but if he'd caught wind of the fake fiancée nonsense, he wasn't commenting on it. "Yeah, I'm off to convince him to let the fireworks show go on. Now that it's not a matter of money, I think he won't give me such a hard time about it."

"Where are you getting the money for the fireworks?" Samantha asked.

"I'll go door-to-door asking for donations, if I have to." Kayleigh grinned. "I've already got two businesses contingent on convincing Evan and Liam to let me do this."

"How are you going to convince Evan?"

"That depends on how unreasonable he's being."

Samantha shot a glance at their father, but he didn't notice. Yeah, Dad didn't know about the fake fiancée proposition. She'd let Samantha break that to him. As Kayleigh was walking out of the shop, a woman and her middle-school-aged son stood up to speak to her.

"They'll be right out." Kayleigh jerked her thumb back at the office. Then she stopped in her tracks, recognizing Chris Danvers and his mother, Mina.

"We couldn't help overhearing what you and your father were talking about," Mina said.

"Hi," Kayleigh said. She wasn't sure how this conversation was going to go, but she was prepared to respectfully listen.

"Chris and I were surprised to see that the fireworks show had been cancelled this year."

"Was it because of me?" Chris asked. His eyes were wide, and his lips were trembling.

Oh, please don't cry. The way she felt right now, she'd be joining in.

"Not really," Kayleigh said quickly. "The factory where we usually buy our fireworks from got flooded out and then during the cleanup, they were hit by looters. We'd already sent them a deposit, which I hope we get back from the insurance. But in the meantime, there wasn't much money, and there was nowhere else that could supply us with fireworks, without going to the roadside stands. And the first selectman didn't want to do that. So they decided to cancel and use the remaining money to help the community. But as you heard, I'm still hoping to put on a show on Saturday night."

Mina said, "You have our support. Chris loves fireworks and he's not alone. I don't want any other kids setting them off and risking themselves. I'd like to donate."

"Great," Kayleigh said. "I need to get the first selectman and police chief on board and then I'll take your donation."

"Can I help?" Chris asked.

"If your mom doesn't mind." Kayleigh glanced up at Mina. "You can help me out by getting your friends and their families to sign a petition about reinstating the fireworks show. I can present it to the first selectman, so he knows what his constituents want." And to the police chief, if he decided to be stubborn.

"I can do that," Chris said.

Kayleigh shook his hand, glad that he had his whole hand.

Her next stop was Evan's house. His car was in the driveway, so she went up and knocked on the door.

"Kayleigh?" Evan peered over her shoulder, looking for someone else. She wasn't sure who. Maybe her sister.

"Got a second?" she asked.

"You're not going to dunk me in a pool, are you? I'm surprised Leah didn't drown me."

"No, I'm here to talk to you about the fireworks show."

He rolled his eyes. "I thought we were past this."

"You were. But I'm not. This show means a lot to this community. And now that it's not affecting your budget, I'd like your blessing to put it back on the agenda."

"With what money?"

"With the money I've collected from private donors who want to keep the tradition alive."

Evan considered her words. "Where are you getting the fireworks?"

"I'm bringing a permit holder to Pennsylvania to buy the shells."

"Who's your permit holder?"

Kayleigh crossed her arms over her chest. "An army buddy of mine. His name is Beck Carver. He's an ammunitions expert. He can buy them, transport them, and set them up. The insurance and responsibility will be on his policy and not the town's."

"Why is he doing this for us?"

"Because I asked him to, and told him it was important to me." Kayleigh had also told Liam how important this was to her, more than once, but that hadn't been enough to get him to agree to the show. And it should have been.

"Did Liam agree to this?"

"Not yet, but he will."

"I'll let that go for now. Is this safe?"

"Yes," Kayleigh said. "I'll make sure it's a safe display. Beck is a licensed shooter, so he'll rig it all up to go off electronically. I'll have the fire department on standby and we'll make sure that there aren't any unexploded shells. We'll set it up and clean it up."

"Can you do this without getting hurt? Without anyone getting hurt?"

"Yes. Beck will see to it. He's had his share of experience

with explosives. So have I."

Evan nodded. "Yeah, I guess we're not teenagers anymore."

"No, but we can have a moment from our childhood when we enjoy the fireworks show."

"It seems so silly."

"It might seem silly to you, but you wouldn't cancel Santa Claus riding in on his sleigh for the Christmas parade, would you?"

"Of course not. The kids would be so disappointed."

"This is the same thing. I'm not saying the fireworks are that big a draw, but it's still magical. If I can raise enough money for a decent show and Beck is here to set them off safely, can we put it back on the agenda?"

"You're still going to have to get the chief of police to agree to this."

"It would be easier if you told him it was back on the agenda. You're his boss."

"It's his town, too, and he needs to make sure we're all safe. If he says it's safe, I'll give my blessing."

"So, you're still putting this all on Liam?" she said. "That's not fair."

"It was our original deal. He has to sign off on the explosives coming into his town."

"Fine," Kayleigh said, exasperated. "If he agrees to my plan, the fireworks display goes back on the agenda?"

"As long as everything is aboveboard and legal."

"It will be." Next time, she was going to bring frogs. It made convincing Evan of things easier. Too bad that wouldn't work with Liam. What could she possibly do or say to him that would change his mind about the show? She'd tried everything. She couldn't even get him to go out on a date with her without it ending in disaster. How could she convince him that the fireworks wouldn't end the same way?

Maybe Beck would have some ideas. She called, but he didn't pick up, so she left him a message. Once she was home, she sat down on the floor and attempted to put together one of the chairs. Kayleigh tried to make it fun by pretending it was a puzzle for adults.

When Beck called her back, she explained the situation to him. "I'd be happy to talk to the chief about his safety concerns."

"I'm not sure that's where the blockade for Liam is."

"You mentioned that he didn't want the extra work. What if we call in some extra security for that event?"

"It's short notice, and I'm not flush with cash."

"You're flush with favors, then. I can get five vets to handle the fireworks site. That leaves the local police to their regular patrols."

"That might work." Kayleigh narrowly missed hammering her finger into the chair. She tossed the hammer aside. She didn't have the brain for this today. "How soon can you get here?"

"Depends. Are the bluefish running?"

"I'll have Leah save you a seat on the boat."

"I'll see you tomorrow, then."

Kayleigh hung up, feeling better about her plan. This was a no-lose scenario. So why did she feel that it was still going to end in a disaster?

Chapter Seventeen

L IAM WAS TRYING to think of the next step he should take with Kayleigh. Dinner seemed to be cursed. Hanging out at the summer festival had been nice. It brought back old memories of when they were kids. And he had really liked dancing with her. He had a feeling that they needed some time away from the crowds, though. A movie would be quiet, but they'd just be sitting next to each other in the dark. Then there was the matter of working out a time when they were both off duty. He wished this was easier.

"Pulled over a Jersey driver in a Mercedes today," Bill said, coming into the station to punch out for his shift.

"Good for you," Cindy said. She was just coming in. "What was he doing?"

"Well, let's just say I told him ninety-five was the road he was on, not the speed limit."

Liam looked up. "That's one hell of a ticket."

"I let him go with a warning."

"Why?" Liam asked.

"He said he was in town to see an army buddy of his. Asked me if I knew Fire Chief Baker."

"We don't give special favors for friends," Liam said sternly.

"He did three tours in Afghanistan."

Liam looked away. He probably would have let a veteran off with a warning too. "Aside from the excessive speed, he was driving safe?"

"Yeah, Chief. The way the car sounded, I doubt he even realized he was going that fast."

Liam grunted. "He'd better keep his lead foot in check while he's in town."

"What did he look like?" Cindy asked.

"How the hell should I know? What kind of question is that?" Bill asked. "He looked like a guy."

"I'm just wondering how close a friend he is to Fire Chief Baker, and what he's doing in town."

"Cut the gossip and get to work, please," Liam said.

Cindy shrugged and went out on patrol.

Liam picked up his keys. "What color was that Mercedes?" he asked Bill.

"Black as night."

Liam grunted again.

After driving around town for a bit, Liam found a black Mercedes with New Jersey plates in the marina parking lot. Leah Baker's boat wasn't in its slip. Maybe Kayleigh's friend was in town for the summer festival, although it was nearing the end. He couldn't shake the feeling that Kayleigh and her army buddy were up to something. His eyes slid to the trunk of the Mercedes. Fireworks were illegal in New Jersey, so there was only a slim chance he was carrying them. Bill didn't mention that he'd searched the car, and he wouldn't have on a routine traffic stop—especially when the army buddy mentioned Kayleigh. Liam ran the plate. It was registered to former army specialist Beck Carver, current residence New Jersey. He owned a security firm. Rent-a-Cop type of place. No priors.

When he got back to the police station, Liam was surprised to see Kayleigh coming out of the building. He flicked on the siren for a moment to make her jump. She glared at him and he grinned back.

"Where's Lead Foot?" he asked.

"Beck said he got pulled over. Thanks for not giving him a ticket."

"Don't thank me. Thank Bill." He parked his car and got out to talk to her. "Tell me that there's not a trunkful of fireworks in that Mercedes."

"There's not a trunkful of fireworks in that Mercedes."

He narrowed his eyes at her.

She narrowed hers back at him. "Can we not fight about fireworks for one day?"

"You tell me. What are you doing here anyway?"

"I wanted to ask you out for lunch, but you weren't here."

"I'm working," he said regretfully. "Why aren't you out on the boat with Leah and Lead Foot?"

Kayleigh cocked her head. "How did you know that's where they are?"

"I'm a cop. It's my job to know things." Liam shrugged. "Besides, it's hard to miss a Mercedes with out-of-state plates."

"I would have liked to go bluefishing with them today.

The bunkers were running. You should have seen them boiling out of the water. My dad dumped all his work on Samantha to go out with them. I've got to work today too. This was my lunch break. Are you coming or what?"

"Sure," Liam said. "Let me tell the crew I'm going out and check my desk. Where do you want to go?"

"How about the Lobster Dock? Lobster dogs on me."

"Throw in fries and you got a deal. I'll meet you there."

Kayleigh smiled and something inside Liam brightened. They usually didn't do lunch together. Heck, they barely hung out unless it was in the line of duty. Maybe this was the start of something new between them. Lunch was a casual affair, so he wouldn't have to bring flowers. Everyone was working, so they would be relatively alone. Finally, something was going his way. He practically danced up the stairs. Just as he was about to walk into his office, he heard Ada say something that stopped him in his tracks.

"Did you see the pictures that Jules put up on Facebook of the two of them? He's an old softie. You can really see how Liam feels about her when he doesn't think anyone is watching them." Ada sighed. "It's so romantic."

Oh, no, it was happening again. The town was creating another story about him and Kayleigh.

"I don't like that she's using his crush on her to manipulate him into signing off on the fireworks show," one of his officers said.

Liam froze. He knew he should walk in and put a stop to the gossip, but he wanted to hear what came next.

Someone snorted. "I don't see what the big deal is. It's

not the town's money she's using. Everyone wants to watch the fireworks. So what if it's not the big deal it used to be?"

"The big deal is the chief said no, and she's not taking that for an answer. I think the timing of this army buddy is a little suspicious, don't you? Now, all of a sudden, Kayleigh comes in here and wants to take Liam out for lunch? Can you say distraction?"

"You think she's going to try to get him to sign off on the fireworks?"

"I think if Liam doesn't, they're going to set them off on Leah's boat just out of the Guilford jurisdiction. That way, they don't need the first selectman or the police chief to approve it."

Liam rested his forehead on the door jamb. How stupid could he be? That's why Lead Foot and Leah were out there. They were looking at places to set up. Depending on the tide, they could even set them up on a sand bar or a flat rock formation. That was crazy dangerous, and he couldn't let it happen.

He had refused to go to Pennsylvania to pick up the fireworks for her legally, so she'd called in a favor to have an army buddy do it for her. This would not stand. He stormed into his office, and Ada and Zach looked at him warily.

"I'm going to lunch with Kayleigh." He glanced at the latest updates on his desk to make sure there weren't any new developments with the break-ins. There was a report about a U-Haul and some of Tristar's fireworks, but he couldn't read it now. Toggling on his Bluetooth, he walked out of the office, then contacted Cindy and told her to go down to the marina and wait for the owner of the Mercedes to come back, and then ask him to open the trunk.

"If he gives you a problem, detain him and call me."

"Yes, Chief," she said.

Liam was still seething when he pulled into the Lobster Dock. Kayleigh was out on the patio and waved her lemonade at him.

"I took the liberty of ordering because I figured you were tight on time."

Liam sat down at the table and saw that there were two lobster dogs and fries waiting for him. Kayleigh had started without him and was down to one.

"Thank you," he forced himself to say.

"What's the matter?" she asked.

He didn't want to notice how pretty she looked with her hair down from her usual ponytail and she had a hint of eye makeup around her dark brown eyes. Liam was too angry to get into this with her now. Instead, he took a bit of his lobster dog, enjoying the bun that was crisp with butter.

"This is good," he said reluctantly, around a mouthful.

"First of the season always tastes special." She smiled, and he didn't want to notice that she had on a soft lip gloss that made her lips look kissable.

After he finished the first lobster dog, his anger was tamped down enough that he decided to give her enough rope to hang herself. "So, why did you invite me out here for lunch?"

She shrugged. "I thought it would be nice to spend some time together."

"And it had nothing to do with fireworks?"

"What's with you today and fireworks? Did you talk to Evan?"

"What's your army buddy really doing here?"

Sighing, Kayleigh nibbled on a French fry. "You really want to talk about fireworks today, don't you?"

"You're darn right I do."

"Fine. I have private donors who are willing to fund the fireworks display. It's costing the taxpayers nothing."

The lobster roll in his gut rolled around. Liam hated being right.

"All I need is for you to tell Evan that you're fine with the show going on as planned."

"But I'm not," Liam said.

Kayleigh blinked. "But the money—"

"It was never about the money. It was about safety and noise violations and prosecuting people in possession of illegal fireworks." He felt a grim satisfaction saying the last part.

"The show will be safe, done before eleven p.m. and all the fireworks will be legally obtained." Kayleigh looked at him. "What is your actual problem with this?"

"My problem is that I told you no and you went over my head."

"How can you be mad that I spoke to Evan? He's the one who's still hiding behind you. You can make or break the fireworks display."

"And what happens if I still say no? Are you going to force me to arrest you?"

"No," she said. "Although, up until this moment, I didn't think you would."

"You broke the law."

"I did not." Kayleigh reared back in offense.

It was a good act. He had to give her that. "You know, you're right. You had your friend do it."

"Do what?"

"I'm going to ask you again and this is your last chance."

"For what?"

"What is Beck Carver doing in my town?"

"He's a licensed shooter. I called him in to rig the fireworks to go off electronically."

"Gotcha," he said. "What fireworks?"

"The fireworks I'm going to buy with the donated money from the people of Mulberry."

"And how are you going to do that without a permit?"

"Beck has his permit."

"But he doesn't have permission to bring fireworks into Connecticut." Liam said.

"Well," Kayleigh said. "That's—"

"And the fireworks I confiscate from his trunk will be used as evidence in his arrest."

She gaped at him. "He doesn't have fireworks in his trunk."

"For his sake, I hope not. But as soon as he gets back from the boat ride with Leah, Officer Hershel will have him pop his trunk."

Kayleigh got a calculating look in her eye, and it threw Liam off his game. "How about we make a bet?"

"I can't wait to hear this."

"If there aren't any fireworks in his trunk, you'll tell Evan that you have no problems with reinstating the fireworks show on the summer festival agenda."

It was in that moment that he knew they'd off-loaded the fireworks.

"So the fireworks are already on the boat? Or are they in your father's garage? Or at one of your houses?"

"Liam," she said, sagging in her seat. "I haven't bought the fireworks yet or told Beck to buy the fireworks. There aren't any fireworks. You've got an obsession."

"You'd know." It probably wasn't his best comeback, but she'd thrown him for a loop and this fight didn't feel like one of their bickering matches. This fight hurt and drew blood, and he wondered if they'd ever come back from this.

"If you don't find fireworks on my family's property, what's next? Are you going to go after my friends? Look under Quinn's doghouse or Ayesha's crib?"

"I'm not going to give you permission to hold a fireworks display in this town, no matter how many lobster dogs you buy me."

"Lunch wasn't about fireworks until you made it about fireworks."

"Whatever," Liam said. He tossed his napkin on his plate and walked out of the restaurant.

Chapter Eighteen

KAYLEIGH TOOK HER family out for dinner at the Leaning Tower of Pizza to make up for the craziness of the day. While Liam didn't search her sisters' homes and businesses, he did send officers around to question them. And he did have Beck open his trunk. The only thing in there, aside from a spare tire, was a duffel bag filled with gym clothes and boxing gloves.

"What's his deal?" Beck asked. He refilled her father's wineglass and then topped everyone else's glass off. Kayleigh could tell that her father and Beck had bonded on the fishing trip. They'd caught a bunch of bluefish. Leah had made them clean and filet them on the boat. Then she coated the filets with panko and fried them up for their lunch. And they didn't save Kayleigh any.

Kayleigh shrugged. "I don't know. He's so angry that I still want to have the fireworks display and he doesn't."

"Well, I'm going to stay at a hotel in the next town over."

"No, don't," Kayleigh said. "You can stay with me."

"Liam wouldn't like that," Leah muttered.

"I don't care what Liam would like," Kayleigh argued. "Not when he's behaving like this."

JAMIE K. SCHMIDT

"I don't want any trouble with the local police," Beck said. "I'll hang around until Saturday just in case you need me, but I don't want to be on his radar."

"You're still coming out fishing, right?" Leah said.

Thunder rumbled in the distance and the light rain came down heavier.

"If the weather clears. Every day, if you'll have me."

"It's the least we can do," Leah said.

"Thanks," Kayleigh said to her sister. "I don't know what's gotten into Liam."

"I think he's jealous of Beck," Samantha said.

Beck and Kayleigh exchanged looks. "Why?"

"Jealousy isn't rational. But Beck smokes into town in a Mercedes and just happens to have a fireworks license and a permit. Liam might be feeling a little inadequate."

"That's ridiculous," Kayleigh said. "I've known Liam all my life. He's never ever been jealous or inadequate."

"Maybe he didn't need to be until now."

Kayleigh shook her head. "He still doesn't need to be. No offense."

"None taken, Sarge," Beck said. The waitress came over with all their salads and they dug in. Kayleigh was looking forward to her lasagna, but she supposed it wouldn't hurt her to eat a vegetable or two after all the fair food she'd been indulging in.

"If he's jealous," her father said. "That means he thinks of you as more than just a friend. And I think you feel the same way."

"I do, but there's Irene Mulberry."

"He's not involved with Irene." Her father shook his head.

When her phone rang, she hoped it was Liam calling to apologize, but it was Phyllis. "What did Quinn do now?" Kayleigh asked.

"Nothing, thank goodness. I don't see your car in the yard. Are you out?"

"Yeah, do you want me to pick you up something?"

"I don't feel like cooking. Are you at a restaurant?"

"Yes, I can pick you up dinner, but I don't know how late we'll be."

"It doesn't matter. It saves me from having to go out."

"Okay. How does manicotti sound?"

"Wonderful, dear. Thank you. I owe you one."

Kayleigh flagged the waitress down and put in Phyllis's order.

"What did he say when you said you would provide your own security?" Beck asked, taking a garlic knot out of the breadbasket.

"I didn't even get that far," Kayleigh said. "He was convinced that we smuggled in fireworks."

"I could have," Beck said. "But I'm glad I didn't."

"Me too. In addition to you being arrested, I don't think Liam would have ever spoken to me again."

Not that they had a lot of things to say to each other now.

Making a face at her phone, Kayleigh put it in her pocket. She'll deal with Liam tomorrow. Right now, they both needed some time to cool down.

LIAM KNOCKED ON Evan's door.

"I was wondering when you'd show up," Evan said. He was dressed in a robe and slippers, but he had a margarita in his hand. "Do you want one?" Evan waggled the glass at him.

"No, I'm on duty."

"Have you come to interrogate me on hiding illegal fireworks in my swimming pool?"

"Are you hiding illegal fireworks?"

"No, and unless you have a warrant to go looking, you can take a hike." Evan made shooing motions.

"I'm actually not here about fireworks."

"Well, that's a switch. Come on in." Evan opened the door wider and Liam walked in. The ionic columns in the front of the house gave the impression it was a mansion, but inside, it was smaller than it looked.

He followed Evan into the parlor and sat down in a comfortable recliner that had seen better days.

"Should I get out the Xbox?" Evan asked, sitting on the couch and putting his feet up on a padded hassock.

"Feel like getting beat at Madden?"

Evan snorted. "In your dreams."

Liam was surprised at how much he wanted to play. When was the last time he had taken some time off for himself?

"Why are you here, Liam? Official business?"

"I want to know what Kayleigh said to you about the

fireworks and this Beck Carver guy."

"Why don't you ask her?"

Looking anywhere but at Evan, Liam said, "We kind of had a fight and I'm afraid she's going to tell me to jump in the lake."

"She said that Beck was a friend of hers from the army that owed her a few favors. He has the necessary permits and licenses to buy, transport, and run a professional fireworks program. They had private donations to pay for the fireworks and she wanted me to put it back on the agenda for the end of the summer festival."

"How much money did she raise?" Liam asked.

"I didn't ask."

"Were there a lot of people who still wanted to have the show?" The fight had narrowed down so much—to just Kayleigh and him—that it was hard to remember that even his own mother had wanted the show to go on.

"I didn't ask."

"Well, what did you contribute to the conversation?" Liam asked, exasperated.

"I said if you thought it was safe, it was fine with me."

"Why are you putting this on me?"

"Because," Evan said, "the town has no liability. This Beck Carver comes with his own insurance. The money doesn't come out of the town budget. That leaves only your department in the mix and you already said you didn't want to have the extra work."

Liam stiffened. "I'm not shirking my duties."

"I never said you were. No one is saying that. If the flood

and theft hadn't happened, we wouldn't be having this conversation. But because it did, I thought we could all take a break. My mistake was not convincing Kayleigh that this was a good thing before taking the fireworks off the schedule."

"What do you want me to do?" Liam asked.

"Kayleigh texted me a solution earlier. I now know why she didn't text it to you. It seems like the best of both worlds."

"What?" Liam didn't like where this was headed.

"Beck Carver runs a security company. He's offered to bring in a team of ex-military personnel to be on firework duty. That would leave your team to just do your normal daily activities. Kayleigh's happy. You're happy. The town's happy, and that makes me happy."

Liam's body flushed hot with anger and then cold with dread. She couldn't go over his head to Evan. So she'd tried to go around him with Beck. Kayleigh was determined to get her way. And Liam was determined to get his.

"I can handle security in my town just fine." Did she think Beck's group could track down the thieves that were breaking into cars at night? What if they could?

Liam stood up so fast, he got dizzy. "Beck Carver's team will not be needed. Nor will his expertise with fireworks. If this is my decision to make, then I'm backing up your original idea. We'll take fireworks off the agenda for this summer."

Evan nodded as he walked Liam out. "Congratulations," he said when they reached the door.

"For what?"

"You won. You beat Kayleigh."

Liam set his jaw. "That's right."

"How does it feel?"

It didn't feel great.

"Would it have killed you to have bent a little on this?"

"Would it have killed her?"

Shaking his head, Evan closed the door, but not before Liam heard him say, "One of these days, I'm going to knock both your heads together."

Chapter Nineteen

"WHAT A DAY," Kayleigh said, driving back home in the pouring rain. Thunder rolled in, loud and angry, while lightning lit up the sky. At least with all this rain, they wouldn't have to worry so much about kids setting off bottle rockets. There was enough noise and flashing to satisfy the most jaded thrill seeker.

The smell of her leftover lasagna and the manicotti she was bringing back to Phyllis filled the car with good smells, but didn't relief the miasma of disappointment that hung over her. She had zero fun over lunch with Liam. Gone was the flirty guy who'd danced with her at Winston Jones. The trash talker from the chili contest was nowhere to be seen. Kayleigh hadn't even gotten a glimpse of her old friend who'd helped deliver Patty's baby.

Instead, she'd sat across from an angry wooden cut-out of him. She would have had more fun with a plant as a lunch companion. The worst part about it was that she'd only thought they had been fighting about fireworks. But apparently, Liam was holding a grudge for some reason. Was it about the money? Maybe he'd decided that it should have gone to the police department. Maybe it should have. It wasn't as if she had been involved in the discussion.

"It's never going to work," she said to the windshield. They bickered too much. Acted like the children they used to be when they got together. Everything was a competition to be won with them. They were forever fifteen years old. And that was no age to have a lasting relationship.

"He could have at least tried," Kayleigh said. For a moment at the fair, she'd thought they'd been a possibility. But whenever real life stepped in, it all fell apart. She guessed it was easy to be in love during fun times, but it was the challenging ones that tested a relationship.

And they had failed.

This was about the time when she used to pack her bags and head to the next town that needed a firefighter. But the urge to leave had passed and Kayleigh knew that she was going to stick around. Unfortunately, that meant she was going to have to give up on being anything more than Liam's friend.

Gripping the steering wheel, Kayleigh's anger with him grew until she was muttering to herself. She was so distracted by that and the sheets of rain cascading down the windshield, she didn't notice that Phyllis's door was torn off the hinges until she got up on her neighbor's porch and had partial shelter.

Warning bells went off in her head. Hadn't Liam said that Mrs. Murray's house had been broken into this way? Fumbling with the bag that had the takeout order in it, she pulled her phone out of her pocket and dialed Liam. Whatever nonsense they were going through, she still trusted him, and they were still friends.

"Pick up. Pick up," she muttered, hoping he wasn't giving her the silent treatment. Glancing around, she realized the power was out. Not only here, but for the rest of the block too. Dinner had gone on really late and she hoped Phyllis hadn't gone to bed hungry.

"Phyllis, are you all right?"

No answer. She took a hesitant step into the house. It was pitch black. She fired up the flashlight app on her cell phone.

Finally, Liam picked up. "You forget to tell me something?" His voice sounded lifeless and bland.

"Hey, it might be nothing, but send a car out to Phyllis's house. The door is wide open, and the screen door has been ripped off the hinges. The power is out and she's not answering when I call out."

"Where are you?" His voice sharpened.

"I'm inside."

"Get out," Liam snapped.

"In a minute. I'm afraid she's hurt and can't get up."

"Where's Quinn?"

"Not here." Kayleigh took a few steps farther into the house. She knew the place well and padded down the foyer in the pitch dark. "Quinn? Here, boy!"

No ruffs or the sound of telltale claws on the floor. Now she was really worried.

"Kayleigh, you do not know what you are walking into. Get out and let me and my department handle it."

"Phyllis?" she called again. Over the phone, she heard Liam's siren go on. "I didn't say you had to come. Call it in to dispatch." The last thing she wanted was to see Liam right now. They both needed space.

"Get out of the house. Go home and lock your doors."

Adrenaline surged through her, sharpening her senses. Liam was worried, and that meant this could be dangerous. But there was no way she was going to leave Phyllis to that fate. "No. I'm right here. If Phyllis is hurt, I can help."

"Yeah, and if there is a burglar, you're walking into something you could avoid."

"I can handle myself, Liam."

"I'm ten minutes away. Maybe less. Go outside and wait for me."

"I told you—" Kayleigh got hit from behind and went sprawling forward, falling hard on her knees. "Oof."

The phone went careening out of her hands as she hit the floor.

"KAYLEIGH!" LIAM SHOUTED into the Bluetooth speaker. "Kayleigh?"

Fear, icy cold, and anger, blistering hot, warred inside him. Outside, thunder blasted the air, reflecting his mood as the lightning strikes continued.

"Kayleigh, answer me! Damn it."

He was pretty sure he was the closest car in the area, but he toggled on his radio to call dispatch. "I need two units, 10-39, sent to 181 East Street, possible 11-7 and 11-8." The squad cars would come in fast, with lights and sirens, knowing that there might be a prowler and a victim.

Liam swallowed hard. Or victims. "Kayleigh?"

Still no answer.

He hoped there was a good explanation for this, but the dread he felt in the pit of his stomach told him otherwise. He pushed the accelerator down, going too fast for the weather conditions, but he didn't care. What was the last thing he said to her at lunch?

"Whatever."

What if that was the last real thing he ever said to her? Gulping down the emotion, Liam forced himself to focus on the road. He eased off the gas to take a curve more safely. Cars were pulling over for him as he flew by. It didn't matter anymore that his feelings had been hurt about her pretending to be interested in him so she could convince him to rein-state the fireworks.

That's why he had been so upset. It had nothing to do with the fireworks and everything to do with feeling used. He huffed out a laugh that didn't have any humor in it. He couldn't even remember why it was so important that he win the fireworks fight. Who cared? So what if his team had to pull a hard shift that night? So what if there were noise complaints? He could make her smile and bring comfort and happiness to her because she was still grieving her mother and her old life before Iraq.

"You're an idiot," he told himself.

Liam had to swerve fast to avoid a downed tree limb in the road. He overcompensated for the jerk of the wheel and his car fishtailed as he corrected it. Liam had harassed her friends and family and for nothing. Kayleigh hadn't bought any fireworks illegally. She had been waiting for Liam to approve the new plan, which had been to have Beck drive down with her to purchase what she could, and then come back to Mulberry, so a professional could set up the show. Why had he been fighting that? It was the perfect solution, and everyone would have been happy. Liam had let his stubbornness create a wall between them. And now, it might be too late.

"Please," he breathed. "Please let her be all right. I'll buy the fireworks myself if I have to."

He just wanted to see her smile, see that she was unharmed. If he couldn't have anything else, he wanted his friend back. Turning into Phyllis's driveway, he jumped out of the car. Pulling his flashlight and pistol from its holster, Liam ignored the rain and ran for the front door.

"Rye ruv roo," Quinn called and came at him fast from the doorway.

Lightning flashed and Liam saw that he had red on his muzzle, paws and chest. Liam stumbled. "No." He trained the flashlight on the ground and saw splashes of red. Quinn had run through them and there were gory paw prints. Pushing emotions to the back of his mind, Liam stormed into the house. "Police!" he snarled, scanning the foyer with flashlight.

"Liam?" It was Kayleigh's voice.

"In the kitchen." That was Phyllis.

His pulse roaring out of control, he holstered the pistol and led with the flashlight. The two of them were sitting at the table, with candles that had been lit, giving the room an eerie glow. Thunder cracked again and Quinn howled.

Phyllis was calmly eating lasagna while Kayleigh was looking in the cabinet under the sink.

"Who's hurt?" he asked hoarsely.

"No one," Kayleigh said.

He flashed the light over her. She was fine. No blood.

"Stop that." Kayleigh covered her eyes with her hand.

"What happened?" He sank down into a chair.

"I fell asleep," Phyllis said. "And the power must have gone out. I took my hearing aids out because the storm was a doozy. It must have gotten worse while I was sleeping."

"Quinn hates loud noises." Kayleigh stood up. She held a rag and a bottle of floor cleaner in her hand. "He busted out of the screen door and was running around the neighborhood."

"What happened to you?" Liam said raggedly. "Why didn't you answer me?"

"Quinn tackled me from behind. The food I was carrying went flying in one direction, and my phone in another. I still don't know where it is. I was able to save the lasagna, but Quinn got the manicotti."

"Tomato sauce." Liam rubbed his hand over his face. "That was tomato sauce I saw all over the porch and floor."

"Yeah, I'm going to clean it up now."

"Don't bother," Phyllis said. "The manicotti's gone. He'll lick up the rest of the sauce and what he misses, I'll clean up in the morning, when the lights come back on, or it's daylight."

Sirens were getting closer. Liam had forgotten about his backup. Sprinting out to the car, he got on the radio, called the all clear, and sent everyone back to normal operations.

"What happened?" one of his officers asked.

"False alarm. Quinn ripped down the door because of the thunder. I thought it was one of our thieves."

"That dog is a menace."

Liam had to agree. Leaning his head back on his head rest, he listened to the drumming of the rain until his heartbeat and pulse came down to normal. He should go back inside and get a statement from Kayleigh and Phyllis, but it was late. He could do it in the morning. Too keyed up to go home or fall asleep, he stayed in the car until the rain stopped and the bad weather blew back out to sea.

By that time, Kayleigh had gone home. She hadn't even noticed he was still in the driveway when she left. Quinn never came out again, so Liam could only assume he was locked in a room somewhere in the house, hopefully not the one with the open window to the roof. Easing himself out of the car, Liam grabbed his toolbox that he kept in the back seat and went to see what he could do about Phyllis's busted screen door.

Chapter Twenty

THE FIRE ALARM horn woke Kayleigh out of a sound sleep. One horn. Barn fire. How? How could there be a barn fire after all the rain they'd just had? Had it got hit by lightning? Did the hay spontaneously combust? She was groggy. Tired from the summer festival and the nonsense with Liam. And now, someone was banging on her door. Stumbling down the stairs, she opened the door to find Liam leaning against the door frame.

"What?" she croaked.

"If you're responding, I've got my squad car. I'll drive you to the station."

Nodding, she pushed out the door.

"Lock it up," Liam said.

"Right." Kayleigh went back inside, grabbed her purse, and locked the house.

"Where's Beck?"

"He's not getting illegal fireworks," she retorted.

"Okay, I deserved that one."

"He's staying in a hotel in Maddington because you ran him out of town."

"Nice jammies," he said. "Are you sure you don't want to change? Or is Hello Kitty all the rage in firefighter apparel?"

"I'll change at the station. They sent the tanker already." Kayleigh checked her phone. "But they may need the ladder." Kayleigh yawned so hard, she thought her jaw would crack. "You going to put on the lights?"

"Not at this hour," he said. "There's no one on the road to warn we're coming."

She squinted at the dashboard. Four in the morning.

"Why are you here?" she asked, leaning back in the seat. It was nice to have a chauffeur, she thought. It gave her a few seconds more to wake up.

"I waited until after the rain stopped and then fixed Phyllis's door."

"Thank you," she said. "That was nice of you. I should have thought of that."

"Anyway, I heard the call come in. The Delrays' barn is on fire."

"I don't see how."

"It started on the inside. There were horses in there, but they kicked their stalls down. It's a mess."

"Go faster." Kayleigh remembered that she was mad at him. But he had been listening to dispatch and gave her the information that she needed. They were good when they kept it professional. She just had to remember that and stop hoping they could have something more.

"At least you'll get to see the racehorse."

"This isn't the way I wanted to do it."

They got to the station just as the second crew was arriving. Liam dropped her off and then sped off to get to the Delray farm in the Lake Hill area. Kayleigh sprinted for her locker and put on a pair of jeans and a long-sleeved T-shirt. She stuffed her feet into thick socks and got on her gear. She was ready to roll out with the ladder truck.

It took about fifteen minutes to get there and Kayleigh fretted about the fire spreading to the garden or to the farmhouse. Luckily, the torrential downpour they just had would go a long way to containing it. She could see the glow of the fire as they approached it, but Kayleigh was glad to see that the horses were far out in the paddock. They looked panicked, but they were unhurt.

Putting on her helmet and respirator, Kayleigh jumped down from the truck. She toggled on her microphone inside her helmet to speak with Hank, who was coordinating the team inside the barn.

"Structure is a total loss," Hank said. "We're pulling out in a few."

"Where's Honey?" Margaret Delray asked the policemen who were talking with her and her husband. Liam had his flashlight out and was looking under the porch.

"Who's Honey?" Kayleigh asked.

"She's our dog. I can't find her or her three puppies."

Kayleigh looked at the barn. "Could she be in there?"

"I don't know." Margaret started to sob. "How did this happen?"

"We'll find out later. Right now, I'll go in and see if Honey is in there."

"Wait. What?" Liam said.

"It's all right. I'll be in and out."

"Two minutes," Hank said. "I don't trust the support

beams. That hay went up like dry tinder."

Kayleigh activated her tracking device. It was probably overkill. She wasn't climbing up into the hay loft, and it wasn't a large building. But it was good to get into the habit.

"Cooper, you guys see any place where a dog might be hiding?"

"Try the stalls. They weren't on fire, so we passed them by."

She ducked in, feeling the intense heat. It was the way she pictured walking into the center of a volcano would be. The fire was still smoldering on the walls as she walked down the center of the barn, checking the individual stalls. Cooper and Paul were spraying down the back of the barn. Kayleigh looked up and saw what Hank was talking about.

"Come on back, guys," she said. Even though the hayloft was drenched, the wood was bowed by the weight of the wet hay and the burned wood made it shaky at best. She was about to head out when movement in the stall ahead of her caught her eye. There was a terrified golden retriever huddled protectively around her pups. "Honey." Kayleigh hunkered down. "Come here, girl."

Honey whined, but wouldn't leave her puppies. Kayleigh went in and scooped up the three wiggling puppies. "Let's go, Mama." She handed a puppy to each of her team as they hustled out of the barn. Honey still wouldn't budge, so Kayleigh picked her up and started out of the barn when she heard the crack.

"No, no, no," she said.

Honey squirmed and Kayleigh let her go. "Run, girl!" she

said, not far behind her. The barn started to collapse from the back to the front. Kayleigh ran as fast as she could in her heavy gear.

This is why we do sprints in these things.

She cleared the barn, but it felt like a giant punched her in the shoulder on the way out. Suddenly, she was on her hands and knees, and a great weight was keeping her from moving.

"Help me get it off of her," Liam said, suddenly at her side.

With Hank on her other side, they lifted the weight pinning her to the ground. Ricki and Cooper hauled her up.

Someone screamed in pain. And then the world went dark red as fire shot up her whole side. Kayleigh looked over, expecting to be engulfed in flames, but her suit was unmarked. Staggering against Cooper, she saw the large beam that had fallen on her. It was on the ground where Hank and Liam tossed it.

"You all right, Chief?" Cooper asked.

"Yeah, I'm fine. It's just my shoulder."

"Good thing it wasn't your head," Ricki said.

"Thank you for saving my pups." Margaret Delray hugged her around the waist.

"Glad to do it." Kayleigh's legs felt unsteady. "Honey was very brave."

The paramedics hustled over and brought her to the ambulance. "I'm fine," Kayleigh said. But she wasn't. She needed help getting out of her gear and it hurt so much. They made her lie down with an ice pack on her shoulder, and Kayleigh closed her eyes against the pain.

LIAM WAS TRYING to shake just how helpless he'd felt when he heard the wood crack and come crashing down. His entire world froze as Cooper and Ricki dragged Kayleigh up when her legs wouldn't support her. She had taken a bad knock. They took her to the ambulance and helped her out of her gear.

Rushing over to her, he pushed Hank out of his way. "Kayleigh," he said. "Are you all right?"

She was lying down. Her eyes were unfocused, and he had to push down the panicked feeling that he was going to lose her.

"Yeah," she said after what seemed like an eternity. "I had on my respirator. My gear took most of the damage."

The paramedic helped her sit up, holding an ice pack on her shoulder. Kayleigh hissed. Liam saw tears prick at the corners of her eyes, and he would have done anything to take away her pain.

"Chief, I need you."

Both he and Kayleigh looked up, but it was one of his officers who wanted his attention.

"Be right back," he said to Kayleigh.

But it was a while before he could get away. After helping his officer, Liam was waylaid by Sean Delray, the owner, who was white-faced and shaken.

"It was me," he said, looking devastated. "I was out here

smoking after dinner and I thought I'd put the butt out. The wind must have taken it. It must have smoldered for hours." Sean rubbed his hand over his face. "I'm so sorry." His shoulders hunched, and he stared at the smoldering wreck of his barn. "Am I going to jail?"

Liam shook his head. "No, but I think your insurance company isn't going to be too happy with you." He had a hard time not laying into the man. Kayleigh and her team could have been seriously hurt. But the people who'd suffered most today were Sean and his family, so he reined in his temper. Liam hoped the cigarette had been worth it.

The dog and her puppies, that Kayleigh had risked her life for, were all right. After the fire in the barn was extinguished, Sean and his wife, Margaret, took the horses out of the paddock and loaded them into their horse trailers so they could move them to a friend's barn for the night.

Liam walked back over to Kayleigh, who was grudgingly letting the paramedics check her over. She didn't look happy about having her arm in a sling, but her shoulder probably needed the support.

Liam hung back, just taking her in. She was very good at her job. She'd made sure her team knew where she was. And when they'd seen her fall when the beam collapsed, they'd reacted as the well-organized team they were. They'd saved all the animals and aside from a few bumps and bruises, everyone was all right.

So why did he feel like grabbing Kayleigh in his arms and never letting her go?

She had shaken off the blanket they had put around her

and crumpled up the water bottle she'd been sipping on. Tossing it in the ambulance's trash can, she looked as if she was going to head back to her crew. Liam stepped in her way.

"Where do you think you're going?" he asked.

"I'm going to help finish up here," she said.

"They can handle this on their own. It wasn't even your shift. Let me give you a ride home. You should take some Tylenol and put more ice on that shoulder."

He knew she was tired and in pain when she didn't give him an immediate argument. Liam took advantage of that and called over, "Hank, you got this? I'm going to take Kayleigh home."

Hank waved and Liam gently steered Kayleigh in the direction of his squad car.

"I should . . ." she started to say, but then just let it go.

Helping her into the car, he fastened her seat belt, being careful of her injured shoulder. "You scared the hell out of me."

"Sorry," she mumbled. "I had it under control. I've been in worse situations."

"I know, but this was the first time I had to watch you go into a burning building and almost not come out."

"Part of the job. You know that," Kayleigh said.

"Yeah." Liam gently closed the door and went around the car to the driver's side. As he drove her home, he came to a decision. "I know how much the fireworks mean to you."

"Do we have to get into this now? At least wait until we get home, and I can take a shot of whiskey to numb the pain.

No fair fighting with me while I'm distracted."

"I'm not fighting with you anymore."

She snorted.

"At least about this." He took a deep breath. "I'm going to tell Evan tomorrow that the fireworks are a necessary part of Mulberry's summer festival tradition."

"What changed your mind?" she said suspiciously.

"Us," he said. "I don't want you to pretend to be interested in me and take me out to lunch to butter me up so that I'm on your side."

"That's not what happened."

"Well, now there's no need to. You're important to me. The fireworks are important to you. I should have been on your side from the beginning, instead of only thinking of making my job easier."

"You're important to me too."

Liam tried to concentrate on the drive home, but he wanted to know what exactly she meant by that.

"But the fireworks issue is null and void. The money is gone. Sure, we could have a small show based on the donations," she said. "But I don't think that's necessary. I shouldn't have reacted the way I did. I know you and Evan have always had the town's best interests at heart. One year without fireworks isn't going to kill us or kill my mother's memory. I'm sorry if I was acting as if it would."

"You don't have anything to be sorry about." He pulled into her driveway and helped her out of the car. "I'm glad you're not hurt too badly."

"I'm tough." Kayleigh gave him a small smile.

Cupping her face with his hand, he rubbed his thumb over her cheek. "Yes, you are. Do you need me to come in and help you with anything?"

"No, I'm going back to bed. It's been a crazy night," she said.

"More like a crazy week." He released her, but she grabbed his hand.

"Liam," Kayleigh began.

Something like hope kindled with desire inside him.

"I value our friendship."

Liam hid a groan as his feelings were crushed into his shoes.

"But I want more."

He almost didn't hear that because of all the self-recriminations going through his head. "What?"

"It's okay if you don't feel the same. I don't want things to be weird and awkward between us after this."

She was speaking words that sounded like English, but he wasn't comprehending them. "What are you saying?"

"Ugh, you are so dense sometimes. I want to date you. Like go out on a date. No firefighters, no police officers. Just you and me. But not dinner. Let's do something safer, like skydiving."

"Not until your shoulder heals," he said. "Skydiving, that is. I'm all for going to the movies or just spending time with each other."

"We'll always be friends." She captured his other hand. "But I'd like to be something more."

Liam didn't have words, so he just nodded. He leaned in

to kiss her, but Phyllis's porch lights flooded on.

"Kayleigh, is that you?" she said.

Quinn thundered out the recently repaired door to investigate. Liam held on to a sigh.

"Rye ruv roo too," he muttered at the dog, who leaned against his leg so hard, he almost knocked him over.

"Yeah, it's me," she called out. "I'm going to bed."

"Good," Phyllis said. "It's late. Quinn, come back in here." She whistled and, miracle of miracles, the dog listened this time.

"Do you want to come in?" Kayleigh asked.

Liam did. He really did. But he was exhausted and once he was more awake, he had an idea to track down and he didn't want Kayleigh listening in and getting her hopes up if he couldn't pull this off. "Not tonight, unless you need my help with something."

"I'll manage."

"Good." He backed up, not wanting to look away, in case this was a dream, and he'd simply imagined it all.

Even though it was closing in on seven a.m., Liam called his mother from the car.

"Liam, I was hoping you'd call. How are the Delrays?"

"They're shaken up, but no one was hurt. Even the animals are fine."

"I'm glad to hear about that."

"I almost lost Kayleigh tonight." If she had been slower or if the beam had been heavier, it could have been a very different ending.

"What? Is she in the hospital?"

"No, I got lucky. But I'm not waiting any longer. Mom,

Kayleigh is the one for me. She has been since kindergarten. I don't care if she's from the Harbor. She's Kayleigh. You know she's not a gold digger."

"Who said that?"

"Dad."

"That man." Lila sighed. "I like Kayleigh a lot. I was just hoping you'd find someone who you had more in common with."

"Money doesn't matter to me."

"You keep mentioning money, not me."

"Then what do you mean? Our jobs are similar. We've known each other forever."

"Liam, you can't be in the same room together without having an argument. I'm afraid that you're going to spend your whole life fighting, instead of being happy."

He chuckled. "I'd rather fight with Kayleigh than laugh with anyone else."

"I suppose I should have known. Jules Baker's Facebook page has more pictures of the two of you than he does of his cars."

"I was afraid of that." Liam shook his head. "I haven't heard a lot of the gossip. But I know they're talking about us again."

"Let them talk," Lila said. "If Kayleigh is who you want, I'm happy for you."

"Thanks, Mom."

"So do you think Kayleigh would agree to having a big wedding at the country club?"

"You'll have to ask her," Liam said. "Remind me to be out of the room when you do."

Chapter Twenty-One

KAYLEIGH AND HER sisters were putting the finishing touches on her kitchen. After listening to them swear and get angry at each other, her dad had stepped in to assemble the new table and chairs. Samantha was on a stepstool, drilling new holes in the drywall for the curtain rod to go in. Kayleigh hated having her arm in the sling because it made her feel vulnerable, and she hated having only one arm to do things.

Still, it did get her out of doing things like washing the trucks for the parade tomorrow. That reminded her . . . She fumbled with her phone. "Hey, Hank?"

"Yeah, boss."

"Did you get the candy?" Every year, the firefighters would throw candy off the truck into the crowd.

"Yup."

He was a wealth of information. "What did you get? I'm hoping we learned our lesson from last year." Last year, they decided to get packages of gum and they got a lot of complaints from the crowd who got beaned in the head or scraped on the "sharp edges" of the rectangle packaging.

"Candy necklaces in plastic bags."

"Good job," Kayleigh said. That had enough heft that it

would reach the side of the road, be sanitary in case it dropped on the ground, and shouldn't hurt anyone. She rolled her eyes.

"When we were kids, they tossed all sorts of things at us, from gobstoppers to fireballs and no one ever complained about a broken tooth or a sore mouth," Samantha said when Kayleigh got off the phone.

"Times change." Kayleigh shrugged. More so this year, without the fireworks. But the money was going to improve the firetrucks, and even she couldn't argue that it wouldn't be money better spent. Still, her heart hurt at the change. Beck was probably still sleeping at his hotel, but as soon as he got up, she'd apologize to him for having to come all this way out here for nothing.

"How's Patty doing?" her father asked.

"She and baby Ayesha are doing great." Kayleigh smiled. "She's so cute. I just want to kiss her little cheeks all over."

"I've got to get busy finishing her baby blanket," Samantha said.

"Don't worry, it's July. I don't think she's going to need it until Christmas."

"It'll be here before you know it."

"Da-ad," they all said at once.

"Don't rush the summer. It just got here. I'm not ready to shovel snow yet." Kayleigh lifted her arm in the sling and winced at the jabbing pain in her shoulder.

"Do you want to take the boat over to New Haven and watch their fireworks tomorrow night?" Leah asked.

Did she? Part of her just wanted to come home after the

parade and rest up in case they were called out again on another fire. Technically, she was on light duty for the next week, but if her family thought she was going to sit home while the rest of her team went out on a call, they didn't know her very well.

"I don't know," she said. "My shoulder hurts."

Leah blinked at her in surprise. "So what? Take a Tylenol and suck it up."

Kayleigh should have known not to expect sympathy from this family. "I got a barn dropped on me."

"And yet, you're still here. Last time that happened, ding dong, the witch was dead," Samantha said.

Kayleigh stuck her tongue out at her.

"Girls," their father warned, but without heat. "Be nice. So what's Liam doing tomorrow night?"

"Why?" Sometimes she wondered if her father had her house bugged. He seemed to know all the details of her life before anyone else did. "He's probably working." Liam was always working. He was a bigger workaholic than she was. And that was saying a lot.

"He was zipping around town all morning, and he and Evan were arguing about something. I was wondering if he had confided in you."

"Nope. He did tell me last night that he had changed his mind about the fireworks display. Maybe that's what he and Evan were fighting about."

"That's great," Samantha said, putting up the kitchen curtains with Leah's help. "Maybe there will be fireworks in Mulberry tomorrow night after all."

Kayleigh shook her head. "No. I'm not going to be able to collect the donations and drive down to Pennsylvania and back with Beck in time."

"I'll go with Beck," Leah said.

Kayleigh wondered if her sister was developing a crush of her own on Beck.

"Who has time for that?" Samantha hopped down from the counter where she was sitting.

"I'd make the time for a ride in that Mercedes."

Kayleigh coughed and glanced at her father, wondering if Leah meant that as a euphemism for something else.

"I've decided to stop fighting for the fireworks. It wasn't making anyone happy. Mom wouldn't have wanted this. It was enough that Liam understood how important it was to me."

Her father nodded.

Kayleigh thought she should let her family know about what she and Liam had discussed last night before things got too out of hand. "But there is one good thing that's come out of all the firework arguments."

"Oh?" her father said, his eyes twinkling.

He knew. He had to know. "Do you want to tell them?" she said exasperatedly.

"Liam and Kayleigh are officially a couple."

Kayleigh wasn't sure on the official part of that, but she didn't correct him.

"It's about time," Samantha said, without sounding surprised.

"How do you know?" Leah asked her father.

"Because I also have an announcement."

Looking at her sisters, Kayleigh wondered what it could be, and why he looked so happy. "What?"

"Irene and I are officially a couple now as well."

"Irene Mulberry?" Kayleigh gasped.

"Dad," Samantha said, sitting down at the table.

"Knew it," Leah said.

"You did not," Kayleigh said. "You thought Irene and Liam were an item."

"I thought it was possible."

"So is her daughter, Karla, going to be our stepsister now?" Samantha asked.

"Whoa, wait a minute. We're dating. Let's take it one step at a time." Her father held up his hands.

"Remember that," Kayleigh said, wagging her finger at him. "When you start with the grandchildren nonsense."

"Yeah," her two sisters said in unison. No one had been left unscathed in that.

Just then a car door slammed, and Quinn called out, "Rye ruv roo."

"I wonder who that is?" Kayleigh smirked and peeked out the window. Sure enough, it was Liam coming up the walk.

"Hey," he said, coming in. "The kitchen looks great. It's finally coming together."

She hooked her good arm through his. "A lot of things are finally coming together."

Clearing his throat, he faced the rest of her family. "I'm glad you're all here. This makes things easier."

Kayleigh frowned. He sounded so serious. That couldn't be good, could it?

"They found an abandoned U-Haul in New Jersey on the side of the road the other night. The serial numbers of the fireworks matched the numbers from the ones stolen from Tristar. We have no perp. The U-Haul had been stolen too. So, because it's not evidence, those fireworks were going back to Tristar. I made a few calls. Had it out with Evan. And Tristar is going to keep our twenty-five-thousand-dollar deposit in exchange for these confiscated fireworks. They're on their way to us." Liam turned to face her. "The Johanna Baker Memorial Fireworks Show will go on tomorrow night—same show, but with a new name."

Blinking back tears, she hugged him the best as she could with one arm. Her sisters piled on and even her father knocked him a few times on the back for good measure.

"I can't believe it," she said, laying her cheek on his chest.

"I'm just glad it all worked out," Liam said.

"Did Evan give you a hard time?"

"He would have, if Chris Danvers and his family hadn't come in with me with a signed petition to keep the fireworks show. It wouldn't have happened without your hard work and commitment to this project."

"Well, come on. We've got to talk to Beck and make sure he'll set up the electronics the way we want it, to go with the music I picked out for Mom. And you owe him an apology." Kayleigh tugged on his arm.

"I guess I'll see you guys later," Liam said.

"Come back for dinner in the new kitchen," Samantha said.

Liam blanched. "I don't want to jinx anything."

"We even got a chair for you." Leah smirked, pointing to the extra one.

"We're going to hit the fair for some turkey legs and baked potatoes," Kayleigh said quickly. "I don't think the kitchen is ready to cook a family meal yet." No need to scare Liam off this early in their budding relationship.

Slumping in relief, Liam nodded. "That seems like the safest choice."

Chapter Twenty-Two

KAYLEIGH AND LIAM lay side by side on the bow of Leah's boat, watching the fireworks from the middle of Mulberry Harbor. The boat was anchored, but the slight wind made it drift slightly, so their vantage point shifted slowly. Small waves lapped at the boat as the thunderous boom of the fireworks sounded and resonated inside Kayleigh's chest. They had the AM radio tuned to the music she and Beck coordinated to go off with the fireworks.

"I should be there," she said sleepily.

"Hank and the others know what they're doing. Beck did a great job." Liam reached down to hold her hand. They had set off the fireworks safely at the fairgrounds, like they had every year since they were kids. They could be seen all over Mulberry, but out here on the water was his favorite place to be. Of course, the next best thing was to be right in the thick of it.

"Are you regretting coming here with me?"

"No." She squeezed his hand. "It's just hard to take a night off."

"I know how you feel. I'm wondering what crimes are being committed while I'm enjoying this moment with you."

"You also have a good staff. They're on top of things."

And they were. In fact, they even had three hoodie-wearing suspects in custody. One of his officers had caught them walking back to their car, and home security cameras confirmed the theft of the handbags they had taken. The town of Mulberry shouldn't see any more thefts as long as they kept their doors locked and a new crew of thieves didn't decide to take up residence.

The sound of laughter from the back of the boat drifted up to them. Her dad and Irene were there with Leah, Samantha, Irene's daughter, Karla, and her boyfriend.

"I guess a part of me wonders if I'm really needed."

"I need you," she said and blushed at Liam's smile that was so full of promise and mischief.

"It's always been you for me," he said. "I'm sorry it's taken me so long to act on it."

"Doesn't matter. You're here now."

"Break it up, you two," Leah said, walking toward them. She carried a bottle of champagne and two plastic wineglasses. "It's almost time for the finale."

They sat up and accepted the glasses while Leah poured them a healthy portion.

"Happy Fourth of July," she said, swigging out of the bottle.

"Happy Fourth," Kayleigh said, tapping her glass to her sister's before Leah went around to the stern again. Kayleigh turned to Liam, who was leaning back on one arm. She watched the bright colors reflect off his face and smiled. "Thank you for making this happen for me. I know you really didn't want to do it."

He caught her gaze with his. "It was important to you, so it became important to me. It's easy to let traditions slip away, but sometimes that's not the best thing for a community or for ourselves. Johanna left behind more than just the festival fireworks and an incredible chicken cacciatore recipe. She was a dear friend and a beloved mother, and if we can share the things she loved, it keeps her memory fresh and alive."

"Exactly," Kayleigh whispered.

"The fireworks mean a lot of things to our town and everyone has a different story or a fond memory. Once I realized all of that, it was an easy enough decision. I'm sorry I didn't see it right away."

"I suppose I could have made it easier on you," Kayleigh said grudgingly.

"When have you ever made it easy on me?" Liam said, with a grin.

"I wouldn't want you to get complacent."

As the fireworks streamed up higher, overlapping each other in noise, color, and spectacle, Liam leaned over and whispered in her ear, "I love you."

"I love you too," she said, and turned her head for a sweet kiss.

The fireworks peaked with an enormous chrysanthemum of white light, fading into a crackling of red, white, and blue sparkles. Then there was silence as the last of the smoke faded into the black of the warm night.

Summer, and their relationship, had both finally begun.

The End

Want more? Check out Trent and Kelly's story in *The Cowboy's Daughter*!

Join Tule Publishing's newsletter for more great reads and weekly deals!

More books by Jamie K. Schmidt

The Three Sisters Ranch series

Book 1: *The Cowboy's Daughter*

Book 2: *The Cowboy's Hunt*

Book 3: *The Cowboy's Heart*

Available now at your favorite online retailer!

About the Author

USA Today bestselling author, Jamie K. Schmidt, writes erotic contemporary love stories and paranormal romances. Her steamy, romantic comedy, Life's a Beach, reached #65 on USA Today, #2 on Barnes & Noble and #9 on Amazon and iBooks. Her Club Inferno series from Random House's Loveswept line has hit both the Amazon and Barnes & Noble top one hundred lists. The first book in the series, Heat, put her on the USA Today bestseller list for the first time, and is a #1 Amazon bestseller. Her book Stud is a 2018 Romance Writers of America Rita® Finalist in Erotica. Her dragon paranormal romance series has been called "fun and quirky" and "endearing." Partnered with New York Times bestselling author and former porn actress, Jenna Jameson, Jamie's hardcover debut, SPICE, continues Jenna's FATE trilogy.

Thank you for reading

A Spark of Romance

If you enjoyed this book, you can find more from all our great authors at TulePublishing.com, or from your favorite online retailer.

TULE
PUBLISHING

www.ingramcontent.com/pod-product-compliance
Lightning Source LLC
Chambersburg PA
CBHW030825020726
47499CB00006B/2074